D0933011

THRONE OF COUNCIL

THE THRONE 3 TRILOGY
THRONE of COUNCIL
Artemis OakGrove

Lace Publications

an imprint of Alyson Publications, Inc.

Copyright © 1986 by Artemis OakGrove. All rights reserved.
Cover photograph copyright © 1991 by Jennie Sullivan.

Typeset and printed in the United States of America.

Lace Publications is an imprint of Alyson Publications, Inc.,
40 Plympton St., Boston, Mass. 02118.
Distributed in England by GMP Publishers,
P.O. Box 247, London N17 9QR England.

Second edition: June 1991

ISBN 1-55583-308-X

All characters in this book are fictional and any resemblance to persons living or
dead is purely coincidental.

Library of Congress Cataloging-in-Publication Data

OakGrove, Artemis
    Throne of council.

    (Lady Winston series) (Throne trilogy; v. 3)
    I. Title.   II. Series.   III. Series: OakGrove,
Artemis.   Throne trilogy; v. 3.
PS3565.A4T5   1986   813′.54   86-21503

I dedicate this book, with all my love, to Karen Hays. I wish also to re-dedicate this entire trilogy to her. If she had not indulged me these last few years I could not have written this story. Although she refuses to take credit, it is truly her work as much as it is mine. She has always been there to encourage me when I thought I'd never write again. Her courage, strength and determination kept me going when my own failed me. Her devotion to me and my creativity not only kept me at it but allowed me to grow as a person. None of this has been easy for her. Like many who are possessed of an artistic temperament, I am moody, demanding, selfish, egotistical and ungrateful. Karen patiently endures all that and more in the name of love — because she thinks I'm worth it. I'm very fortunate to be with this amazing woman. She has worked long, weary hours for several years so I can stay home to write and publish fiction. My fondest wish is that she may some day reap the benefits of all her loving efforts.

The author wishes to thank the following people:

Jasphire, for her devotion and service.
Kat, for hers.
K. S. Koch, for her constant friendship and support.
The IBP, for her intensity and the wonderful carriage ride.
Tibi, for her one woman cheering section.
Hazel F., for her expertise.
Carole T., for her humor and dog-eared pages (*fan* me, Melanie).

TABLE OF CONTENTS

Prologue

Long ago, in the land now known as Ireland lived a small clan of Pagan women. Their beautiful, cruel High Priestess Anara was constantly attended by her protégé and lover, Korian. Also with her every minute were her handmaiden, Fila, and her pet white tigress.

In time, Korian grew discontent, believing Anara unworthy of her honored position. Guided subtly by her mother, Korian obtained the assistance of Lizack, a girl no older than herself, to poison Anara. Lizack agreed eagerly for she was in love with Korian and saw this murder as a pathway to her heart. Once this deed was accomplished, however, her life was forfeit; she was stoned to death by an angry mob of townspeople. Anara's handmaiden, Fila, took her own life to be with her Mistress. Korian was murdered by Anara's white tigress.

Three thousand years later Anara saw her chance to even the score for betrayal of her followers when all of them reincarnated on earth at the same time.

As if returning to the scene of the crime, Korian came back to the physical world in modern day County Donegal, Ireland.

Serving notice to all who would assist this traitoress through her path of growth, Anara deprived Korian of her new mother at the onset. To console himself for the loss of his dear wife, Patrick O'Donnell christened his female offspring Ryan — his first official act in a never-ending campaign to create for himself the son he had always hoped for, and with his wife dead had no chance to get any other way.

Fleeing the overbearing pressures applied by his family and Church to raise Ryan as a girl, Patrick immigrated to America, accompanied by his housekeeper, Bonnie, who served as Ryan's surrogate mother. At the behest of his cousin, Sean MacSweeney, whose wife had also borne a daughter on that selfsame day of Ryan's birth, Patrick settled in Denver, Colorado. Sean's daughter, Brigid, was Ryan's closest and dearest friend throughout her childhood and youth.

The soul who had been Korian's mother chose to return to the physical world in Denver as Ryan's destiny and champion, Leslie Anne Serle.

Anara's murderess, Lizack, returned in Kingston, Jamaica as Sanji Charles—the catalyst for many of the tragedies that would befall Ryan after meeting her.

Anara's handmaiden, Fila, "appeared" as Rags, not reincarnated but sent by her Mistress with a mission: find all the members of her erstwhile clan, then break their wills as punishment for their participation in Anara's murder.

Anara preferred to remain in the spirit world where she could observe the proceedings in the physical world with amusement while exerting her great powers as she saw fit to create more trouble and pain for the victims of her plot for revenge.

On the premise that the more someone had the more she had to lose, Anara left Ryan alone for several years. During that time Ryan had an untroubled youth which she shared with her cousin, Brigid. Both were child prodigies and products of Old Money. Ryan became an accomplished pilot, Brigid a master ceramacist. Having more in common than blood and birthdates, these inseparable friends shared a preference for those of their own sex, but, even more binding, was their ability to experience the other's pain. Mercifully, only a watered-down version of Ryan's pain befell Brigid, transmitting no more to her than an acute awareness of it. Ryan, however, was possessed of a wide range of paranormal abilities not the least of which was her empathic faculty. Her encounters with Brigid's pain were as real to her as they were to Brigid.

When Anara began her seige upon her foe it was this vulnerability she chose to capitalize on first. Ryan had everything—a close, loving relationship with her father, a passion for flying, wealth, good looks, an easy way with women, happiness — it was time to start taking it away from her.

On Ryan's twenty-first birthday, she was to experience, via Brigid, more pain than she had ever known. Heavily intoxicated, Brigid had driven into a bridge abutment, seriously injuring her, and damaging her leg so severely that it had to be amputated. After months of recovery, Brigid had still not regained her self-confidence. Her feelings of unworthiness led her to commit the biggest mistake of her life. Rather than pursue her new love for Dana Shaeffer, she introduced the beauty to her cousin, Ryan.

For Ryan, it was love at first sight; she and Dana were wed within a month. It was not a marriage made in heaven. Dana was ambitious, selfish, and demanded more of Ryan's time than she was willing to give. Dana learned, too late, that she could only run a close second to Ryan's first love: flying.

As with all such women, Dana began to look elsewhere for a more suitable mate; she didn't have far to look. Delores Rhinehart, an attorney, was capable of every devotion Ryan was too preoccupied to give, and wasted no time proving it to Dana.

When Ryan was twenty-five, Anara played the next card in her evil game: Ryan's father was killed in an auto accident. Unable to bear Ryan's engulfing grief, Dana left her bereaving spouse for her long-time suitor, Delores.

Devastated, Ryan began to drink herself into oblivion armed with the full knowledge of her body's unusual response to enormous quantities of alcohol. It was just a matter of time before her voluntary muscle control would quit her, she would stop breathing and she would be escorted into the bliss of another existence.

She would have succeeded were it not for the owner of the bar she had chosen to sing her swan song in. Rags, Anara's agent, pulled Ryan from the gutter in front of the bar, revived her, then took her to her own home where she held Ryan captive for two weeks.

Thus began several years of torture, intimidation, rape, and brainwashing. Exerting her own paranormal abilities — reading and manipulating other people's minds — Rags seized control over every aspect of Ryan's life, most especially her flying. Ryan lived with the constant fear that Rags would turn on her as she had on others, beat her beyond recovery, and rob her of her ability to fly. This threat weighed heavily on Ryan, making her prey to Rags' every whim and need. Rags made short order of forcing Ryan into obedient submission but neither Rags or Anara had anticipated the strength of Ryan's will. Unlike the other members of the clan who had been severely beaten by Rags, Ryan's will was not completely broken.

Then Sanji Charles walked into their lives and everything changed. The Jamaican beauty captured Ryan's fancy and Rags' heart the moment she came into the bar. But it was Ryan who captured both Sanji's fancy *and* her heart. Rags and Ryan entered a quiet time in their lives where their ironic comradeship blossomed into a genuine friendship over and above the inhumane nature of the rest of their dealings with one another.

For two years Sanji offered herself up as Ryan's willing and able sex-slave, but was wholly unsuccessful at interesting Ryan in anything more serious. Ryan had never recovered from Dana's betrayal—her heart was cold.

It had been six years since Ryan held felt anything for another woman; she wouldn't allow herself to. She would have gone on suppressing her enormous capacity for love if fate, in the person of a gorgeous attorney, Leslie Serle, had not crossed her path en route to a night of escape, drinking and dancing.

Rags realized immediately that a relationship between Ryan and Leslie would improve her chances with Sanji so took steps to encourage it. Everything conspired against the growing love between Ryan and Leslie: Ryan's fear of letting herself love another woman, Leslie's pride, Sanji's jealousy, the disapproval of Leslie's friends.

Before long, events and emotions collided when Sanji jealously attacked Ryan, breaking two of Ryan's ribs. Later, drunken and enraged, Ryan retaliated by nearly whipping Sanji to death.

Unbeknownst to anyone, Anara had conceived Ryan's attack on Sanji as part of her revenge scheme. Her perverse sense of justice gave rise to the idea that it should be Ryan who should punish the one she had commissioned to murder Anara in her earlier lifetime.

Rags rescued Sanji and took her for her own lover. When Rags discovered that Ryan had wasted no time in sleeping with Leslie she lost her temper and threatened bodily harm to Ryan. To punish Ryan for hurting Sanji, Rags forced Ryan to stop seeing Leslie. To avoid the beating that would occur if she continued any contact with Leslie, Ryan agreed.

Alone and unhappy, Ryan turned to Christine, a teenage girl, for comfort. Leslie's health and work suffered dramatically during their forced separation. It was during this time that Ryan learned her cousin, Brigid, had been friends with Leslie for many years without her knowledge. Brigid made an unsuccessful attempt to get Ryan to plead with Rags for forgiveness, but Ryan did agree to let her take an encouraging message to Leslie.

When Ryan was arrested on morals charges stemming from her relationship with Christine, she turned to Rags for help. By then, Rags had established her relationship with Sanji and felt safe in allowing Ryan to again see Leslie.

Ryan had gained the courage to love again, and happily took up the challenge of resuming her rocky affair with Leslie, the woman who owned her heart.

All was well until Leslie discovered first-hand how brutally Ryan had injured Sanji. Ryan feared that Leslie was so shocked and angered that she would never see her again. She was too proud to ask for forgiveness or ask Leslie to return to her, thus they were separated once again. Ryan found herself unable to seek comfort with other women; she was truly heartsick — and vulnerable.

Dana Shaeffer, however, had over the years grown accustomed to Ryan's inability to love women other than her. When she learned her spell had finally worn off she took steps to recast it. Her plan back-fired and she was left, humiliated and scorned, in the wake of Ryan's need to make her pay for the years of pain she'd caused. Dana vowed to have her revenge against Ryan.

Ryan and Leslie *did* reconcile and planned to marry. After Ryan, Leslie and Rags celebrated this decision at the bar, Rags was murdered by her arch-enemy, a woman who sought to take Sanji from Rags.

Almost immediately after Rags' death, Ryan purchased McKinley Mansion where she and Leslie shared their lives as a married couple.

Anara was tireless in her attempts to ruin their wedded bliss. She teamed up with Dana, and together they chipped away at Ryan's strength and will.

Dana took the indirect approach. She turned her attention to Brigid and succeeded in ruining Brigid's long-standing relationship with her lover, Star. Along with Dana's betrayal, this served to drive Brigid temporarily mad. She was invited to McKinley to recuperate precisely as Anara and Dana had hoped. Every detail of Brigid's illness and pain was visited upon Ryan who suffered along with her. The healing process led to Brigid falling in love with Leslie, again as the schemers had hoped.

Anara's methods were destructive in intent but somehow less successful in purpose. Her ongoing attempts to sever the bond of love between Leslie and Ryan were always counter-productive. When she tried to capitalize on Ryan's sexual weakness for Sanji, Leslie tripped her up by installing Sanji in the household as Ryan's sex-slave. When Anara tried to get Ryan by hurting Christine, the girl who had been Ryan's savioress during her darkest hour, Ryan defied a court order to save Christine's life. Anara's efforts to take advantage of Ryan's pathological fear of cats were underminded by Leslie who was able to trace the night terrors of Ryan's past-life death to their source, her destruction by Anara's pet tigress.

While each individual act of revenge went astray of its original intent, the combined effect gave Anara great satisfaction. When Sanji broke through her memory barrier to recall the whipping incident, and Ryan realized it was Anara who had planned that and all that had gone before, Ryan finally cracked under the strain.

It was then that Anara was her most angry *and* most dangerous. Revenge against her one-time lover was just a game to her — filling the time until she was to fulfill her true purpose. Anara was one of two souls who would do battle, one destroying the other, leaving the victor to ascend to the coveted position of Queen Regent of The Throne of Council, an unchallenged seat of authority whereby, upon acquiring it, the bearer could control and manipulate planetary events for eons to come.

The time of this struggle was fast approaching and Anara had yet to learn who her opponent was. Her rage was all-consuming when she learned, from a traitor on the Council, that she was to fight with her nemesis: her former lover, Korian, who was now her hated enemy, Ryan O'Donnell.

Upon summoning her opponent before her in the spirit world, she learned that her enemy had acquired a name of power, Blaise, and was as ready as she to do battle.

What she did *not* know was the true identity of the current holder of the title Queen Regent—Leslie Anne Serle—whose name of growth in the spirit world was the One Who Seeks Knowledge and Justice and whose name of power (known only to herself, her lover Blaise, and her suitor, the Goddess of Fire) was Venadia. Anara was also ignorant of Venadia's all-consuming interest in the final outcome of the battle.

With a mind to punish Blaise for hiding *her* true identity and humiliating her, Anara unwittingly rekindled her own, three millennium old love for Blaise. Her punishment/seduction transformed into genuinely passionate lovemaking and reawakened Blaise's love for her. Their mutual proclamation of love shocked and hurt Venadia.

Finally, without trying to, Anara had hit upon the one thing that could ruin Ryan's relationship with Leslie: her own dormant love.

1

"Put the knife down, Ryan."

Vic, the seasoned, middle-aged bartender had refereed more fights than she could remember. Normally she counted on her instinct to bring matters to swift conclusions. Rarely, and unfortunately, instinct wasn't enough. When an altercation between patrons of Sergio's Bar *began* out-of-hand rather than threatened to become so, Vic had to also rely on her wits and her personal knowledge of the women involved to prevent bodily harm or bloodshed.

In all her years as Sergio's bartender, Vic had never encountered a brawler more unpredictable than Ryan. To calculate which way the wind was going to blow with Ryan, she had to take into account a number of factors: who else was in the bar, or more importantly in this case, who wasn't there—Rags or Brigid—what Ryan was drinking, the tenor of emotion in the other patrons, and what the fight was about. When she added up the facts—Ryan was alone and drinking whiskey, emotion among the dozen or so other women present was running high, and, worst of all, the fight was personal—the sum was extremely unstable.

Briefly Vic wished Rags were still alive and here right now; *she* could have handled Ryan and her temper. But, Vic reasoned, if Rags were alive no one would have dared voice the rumor that had started this fight in the first place.

The long, dreary room that was Sergio's Bar was nearly silent except for occasional uneasy shifting of feet and Ryan's throaty breath underscoring the deadliness of her intentions.

When Paula, Ryan's opponent, had boldly and loudly asserted that Ryan had been a sex-slave to Rags, Ryan had hurled herself from her place at the bar, over the pool table and attacked Paula. With a swift accuracy that belied her drunkenness she had restrained her accuser by wrenching her arm painfully back and against her shoulder blade.

Surprised, but undaunted, Paula had become immediately aware of the switchblade poised at her throat. Full of liquor and false courage, she was not alert to the exigency of her situation. Even when Ryan had broken the electric silence with a savage demand for a retraction of her slanderous remark Paula remained contemptuous.

But Vic was all too aware of the hazardous situation she was faced with. Her hands were sweating and itching to pick up the telephone to call the police. Unlike some disreputable bars in town, Sergio's enjoyed a watchful truce with law enforcement officers assigned to its beat. All the bars Ryan owned did. Disturbances were ignored unless complaints were filed or the management solicited assistance. Vic had done so a scant three times in seven years and each time several women had been hauled off to jail. Calling the police wasn't the best choice, Vic prayed it wouldn't be the only one.

She had already asked the barmaid to use the phone in the back to make another call: to McKinley, the mansion Ryan shared with her lover, Leslie. In recent weeks Vic had made the request of her barmaid on a fairly regular basis. Each time, an inhabitant of the the massive residence would take the call and, before long, someone would appear to escort Ryan home, where, in Vic's mind, she belonged.

The restless atmosphere in the bar was increasing in intensity. Vic took charge of the agitated crowd by carefully placing herself between their imposing random half-circle and the combatants. She faced Ryan and began to reason with her, using a sure, steady voice.

"Come on now, Ryan. Just put the knife away and let her go. I'll pour you another drink and send Paula home to sleep it off." She didn't step any closer than two armlengths from Ryan

2

who was tall and long-limbed. The fierce Irishwoman had Vic's reach and could easily take a swipe at her to keep her at a distance. The poorly lighted room had prevented her from getting a good look into Ryan's turbulent, jade-green eyes — until now. Ryan, tense and alert, was far angrier than Vic had first realized. Tiny beads of moisture capped her dark, drawn brow. The muscles outlining her finely carved jaw pulsed and tightened. To Vic's well-trained eye all hope of reasoning with her employer had long since vanished. Quickly she mentally reviewed the events that led up to this stand-off to see where she had lost control of the situation.

Paula had arrived at Sergio's with a sufficient amount of booze in her system to seize her opportunity the moment she'd seen it. Barely ten minutes had elapsed, not nearly enough time to assess Ryan's complex mood, before she'd lit into Ryan verbally.

Accustomed to goading taunts from younger butches, Ryan had ignored comment upon comment — seemingly unconcerned. Those who watched were primed for a good fight and some excitement. They, like Vic, had seen no cause for alarm when they noted Ryan's neck muscles tightening under the collar of her bomber-style, black leather jacket.

Because Paula had kept the pool table between herself and Ryan, who was seated at the bar, Vic had mistaken the gesture for one of vague cowardice: the precursor to a normal Saturday night free-for-all. She'd watched Ryan's long, slender fingers clench her whiskey glass tightly but Ryan's back had been to her, hiding the storm that brewed in her powerful eyes. Vic had thought nothing of it.

When Paula had actually accused Ryan of being a sex-slave to the now deceased Rags, everyone had been stunned by the defamatory remark, but even more by the lightning quick response it evoked from Ryan.

Vic wasn't willing to underestimate the matter now. It had all happened too suddenly. Ryan never pulled her switchblade unless she felt it was absolutely necessary: to end a fight quickly or because another had called forth a weapon first. But she had never drawn it simply because she was angry — before tonight. Trying again, Vic approached Paula.

"Paula, listen to me. Just take back what you said and Ryan will let you go. No one will get hurt and you can go home to your old lady and a good night's rest," Vic urged, wishing she felt as certain as she sounded.

Paula was no more willing to back down from her stance than Ryan. She was sure of what she had witnessed, by mistake, one night through the delivery entrance to the now non-existent kitchen of what had then been Cary's Bar. For the last couple years she had been hanging out at another women's bar and hadn't seen Ryan. She hadn't been conscious of any valid or concrete reason to dislike Ryan — only a vague envy of the older woman's confidence, wealth and success with women. Just young enough not to know any better, Paula had wanted to bring Ryan down a peg or two to relieve some of her own, ever-present feelings of inadequacy.

"No way," Paula insisted. The involuntary shrinking of her neck muscles away from the knife at her throat thinned Paula's voice. "I know what I saw. Ryan was . . . aahh!" Her shoulder had come out of its socket and gone sharply back in again when Ryan gave a disjointing yank upwards to keep Paula from continuing with her claim.

Ryan's control was wavering. Her own outburst of anger had given the night to Paula. It didn't take much to see that written in the eyes of everyone around her. If Paula's accusation had had no truth in it, she wouldn't have flown across the pool table, like the seasoned warrior that she was. By attacking the younger woman she had tipped her hand to everyone there.

It was hard enough to have lived through the horror of being an unwilling sex-slave. But to have it be *known* to anyone who was not close to and trusted by her was more than Ryan could bear. She knew she had to put an end to the betrayal, that the laying bare of her soul could go no further than this room. The feeling of being cornered, trapped, evoked more memories than she could handle.

Without warning, Ryan's expression changed, becoming darker, more focused, waveringly homicidal. The climate took on a lethal quality and those who had been looking for excitement began to back away. They were getting more than they bargained for but their fascination still held them nearby, spellbound.

Vic was about to call the authorities when she remembered something she'd heard one of Ryan's old flames say once. It had been about Ryan needing an offering of some sort to turn the corner on one of her fits of temper.

Since Rags wasn't around to squelch the fire with one well-placed command, nor Ryan's cousin, Brigid, to soft-talk her out of her anger, maybe, if she thought fast enough, Vic could conjure up a symbolic sacrifice to appease Ryan's wrath.

But before she could act in any way, Ryan tightened the knife blade against Paula's skin and voiced a deep, frightening threat. Her statement was so low and thready that only Paula could hear it, hotly in her ear.

"Don't kid yourself, Paula. I've killed before, I'll do it again."

Paula tensed every muscle. Ryan didn't have to tell her that she had caused the death of Rags' killer, CJ. Absurdly, Paula had to know how Ryan had accomplished the feat when she had been miles from CJ's auto crash site. "How?" Paula whispered.

Again, so quietly it was unnerving, Ryan said, "I just *willed* it, and it was."

Something in Ryan's voice told Paula that the nearly forgotten accident hadn't been an accident after all, something she and others had suspected at the time.

Before Paula could decide what to do with that information, Ryan planted a fact firmly in her mind. "Do you think I have to use this knife to take your life? You can suffer the same fate as CJ if you like." Ryan was filled with her own power; it made her light-headed and would have separated her from her body—a state where she was capable of anything—were she not grounded by the sickening, furious disgust she was feeling.

She was left with no alternative but to tip her hand a little further. It had not, as Paula had suggested, been by choice that Ryan had had sexual relations with her formidable friend, Rags. Defeated, but unwilling to let Paula think she deserved much, if anything, in the way of an explanation, she spoke clearly and succinctly. In so doing, however, she left no doubt that her captive was still in grave danger.

"I was *forced* to have sex with Rags. She *beat* me, and *tortured* me, and *raped* me." She emphasized each action word with undiluted hatred. The pureness of her agony was felt by all.

Everyone in the room had known Rags all too well, including Paula. A collective gasp lent credibility to Ryan's revelation. For Vic, the mystery of unexplained blackened eyes, and the feeling that Ryan had always seemed to be in pain, was solved. They had all been afraid of Rags at one time or anther. Ryan's blatant submissiveness to Rags assumed new meaning for each

5

of the women, who looked at one another for confirmation, then back to Ryan with a new measure of understanding.

Even Paula silently conveyed her comprehension by rearranging the muscles in her body from their complicity of challenge into a wave of acquiescence.

Vic took a tentative step forward, hoping that Paula's demonstration of sympathy would be the suitable offering needed to forestall a true act of violence.

But Ryan had grown bloodthirsty in her need for oblation. She had been too insulted and hurt to let the matter drop without exacting her due. She was going to let it be known, once and for all, that the subject was closed.

Paula stiffened suddenly when Ryan spoke again, this time just to her, "You will *never* speak of this again." Paula couldn't believe the stinging flames of pain that scored her neck as Ryan illustrated her command. The razor edge opened several layers of skin in a straight, unmerciful line as Ryan drew the blade precisely across her throat. The wound was not deep enough to be life-threatening, just angry enough to leave a telling scar on skin and psyche. Blood smeared down Paula's short neck like soapy water down a window pane.

There were gasps and hisses all about but no one came to Paula's aid. Everyone stood, waiting cautiously, uncertainly.

Ryan's eyes unfocused, became distant, as she savored the smell of the sacrificial blood she'd drawn. A long, deranged moment passed, suspended in silence. As she returned to reality she became very weak, dropped the knife, loosened her hold on her victim and staggered into the nearest booth.

Vic rushed to Ryan's aid. At the same moment Paula cried out in pain and was smothered by the gathering concern of the other women. The barmaid had the presence of mind to apply a compress to the injury and brush the crowd away from her path to the back room and what first aid she could find to administer.

During the mildly outraged confusion that ensued, Vic managed to settle Ryan into the booth with a whiskey and cigarette. At least she knew her employer *that* well, she consoled herself.

Ryan consumed the drink with one swallow and took a long drag on her cigarette. Exhausted, she exhaled with a sigh and let her head come to rest on her arm on the table, blocking the attentions of her friends. Someone had picked up, wiped off and placed Ryan's switchblade beside the hand holding her ignored cigarette.

Before long someone realized that Ryan had passed out and took the smoldering butt from the crook in her fingers before it burned the flesh.

In response to the call placed earlier to McKinley, Bernie Valasquez arrived in her pick-up truck and walked resolutely into Sergio's. The juke box provided noncommittal background noise leaving patrons free to discuss the event privately among themselves. She discovered two clusters of people: one hovering solicitously around Paula at the bar, the other milling around Ryan as if to protect her from her own pain.

Bernie was deeply concerned when she deduced that a fight with injuries had taken place. She spied Ryan slumped over the table and started toward her but halted when she caught Vic signaling from behind the bar.

A solid, brusque woman, Bernie leaned into the bar counter to receive Vic's confidence. "What happened here? Is Ryan all right?" she asked urgently.

"Passed out. I don't think you'll have to argue with her about leaving tonight. She and Paula," Vic motioned toward the injured party, "got into it. Nothing serious, but she had us all going for a bit. I don't know when I've seen Ryan so angry — if ever." Vic provided the information casually to gloss over the fact that no one was really willing to talk about what prompted the fight — only the fight itself.

Bernie glanced toward Paula who had reassumed the better part of her confident arrogance. But it was only assumed. After forty-five years of hard living, Bernie wasn't fooled. Whatever had gone down between Paula and Ryan had left the younger woman shaken and haunted.

Correctly judging the mood in the bar, she made light of the incident. "Passed out, eh?" she erupted boldly, clapping her peer soundly on the shoulder. "Was a time when only me and you could drink Ryan under the table. Ain't that right, Vic?" Bernie made her comment loud and rowdy enough to engage everyone's attention. She judiciously failed to mention that Rags had numbered among the few who could hold more liquor than Ryan. If anyone noticed, they gave no hint of it.

Vic laughed nervously at first, then let out a solid belly laugh of relief. "You got that right, buddy," she roared.

Bernie deftly caught the can of beer her friend tossed to her, opened it then barked an order to two women to gain their assistance in getting Ryan's chopper into the back of the pick-up. The sudden movement of the two recruits released the remaining tension from the room and everything returned to normal.

The motorcycle secured safely in the truck bed, Bernie came back inside to have another beer and retrieve her friend. She glanced at the clock—just after midnight—and frowned. Ryan's wife, Leslie, would be glad to have Ryan back earlier than normal, but it worried Bernie that Ryan had already had enough to drink that she had slipped into unconsciousness.

"Vic, how much has she had?"

"Too much. She sure can't hold it like she used to." Vic looked sadly in Ryan's direction and shook her head. "Beats the hell out of trying to cut her off though."

Bernie chuckled, imagining the scene: a stubborn bartender trying to keep an even more stubborn owner from drinking more than she should. "I'll bet it does, my friend. I'll just bet it does," she agreed affably as she hoisted herself off the barstool and walked toward her employer. Halting along the way to examine the damage that had been done, she peeked under Paula's makeshift bandage and clucked. "Better have a doctor look at that. Are you gonna press charges?"

Paula turned away from Bernie and toward the bar mumbling, "Just a scratch," and shaking her head "no".

Satisfied, Bernie turned to the task at hand. She picked up the knife, closed it and slipped it into her own pocket. At five foot-ten, Ryan had three inches on Bernie but nothing on her in strength. If it had been anyone else she would have been lifted over Bernie's shoulder like so many potatoes in a sack. But conscious of Ryan's dignity, she roused her friend into a peripheral state of awareness, got her out of the booth and outside where she placed her carefully into the cab of the truck, and softly closed the door. She got in herself and drove away as though she had been sent to pick up a load of groceries.

Once on the freeway, Ryan came to fully and glanced over her shoulder. Seeing her Harley gleaming reassuringly at her as they passed under the streetlamps that lined their way, she turned her stern gaze to Bernie, her full-time mechanic and part-time chauffeur.

Sensing Ryan's stare, Bernie took the knife from her pocket and placed it on the seat between them. "You drew blood tonight, O'Donnell." Her tone was a mixture of the reproach she believed she should express as Ryan's elder by twelve years and the respect normally accorded to someone who has just drawn blood in anger.

Ryan returned the weapon to its usual pocket in her jacket. She continued to stare silently with a defiant, sidelong look.

Bernie's eyes left the road ahead to glance at her dark passenger. She'd known Ryan too many years to think an explanation would be forthcoming but she asked anyway. "What did Paul do?"

"She said the wrong thing." Ryan's terse comeback marked her annoyance. She felt that she had every right to have defended her pride and privacy even if it meant spilling another's blood; it was a small price to pay to call a halt to her public humiliation. The matter was wholly justified in her sight and was best forgotten.

Bernie shook her head slightly in surrender, checked the mirrors to change lanes, then changed the subject. "Your cousin kept late hours again tonight, boss," she revealed letting Ryan know that her red-headed relative had stayed at McKinley longer than what seemed proper. Bernie didn't like it that Ryan left her wife alone so frequently at night. What she liked even less was that Ryan's cousin, Brigid MacSweeney, took advantage of Ryan's absences to call on Leslie. Courting her was a better description, Bernie thought.

Ryan was unconcerned. "Leslie can take care of herself." She knew Leslie was not interested in allowing her friendship with Brigid to become anything more meaningful, and that Brigid's late evening visits were confined to the sitting room of the great mansion.

What she would not acknowledge was that her own relationship with Brigid had deteriorated to the point where they were no longer on speaking terms; that her excessive drinking and irresponsible behavior toward her wife was placing an intolerable strain on their marriage; that she was very near forsaking her earthly existence to permanently rejoin her spirit world lover from a former lifetime.

She was living in a world of denial and everyone could see it except her. This included Bernie who, since becoming Ryan's employee and taking up residence in the servant's quarters, had made frequent attempts to incite Ryan to forbid Brigid's visits.

Ryan wouldn't budge. As long, she contended, as Leslie cherished Brigid as a dear friend she was to be allowed to come to McKinley whenever Leslie would receive her.

Still, Bernie thought it was terribly odd that Brigid always seemed to know when Ryan wasn't around; she always managed to find a way to be alone with Leslie. "You don't think it's funny that she's only there when you're not?"

Ryan thought it was a blessing that Brigid made her appearances while she was away — it was much more comfortable that way. "You have a suspicious mind, Bernie. Aren't you getting enough of what you need in the servant's quarters? Ryan bantered. She liked to tease her friend about the "fringe" benefits of her employment.

Bernie laughed and a gleam came to her eyes when she thought about the young, spunky chambermaid who willingly shared her bed. "Yes, Master Ryan," Bernie needled in reply, "the nicest thing you ever did for me was set me up in the small house."

Ryan's thoughts had turned to her own beautiful bedmate. And lascivious thoughts they were. She returned Bernie's cocky smile and wicked wink with a crude laugh. Placing her booted foot on top of Bernie's, she applied added pressure to the accelerator.

"Get this crate moving, driver," she ordered. "Get me home so I can screw my wife."

"Anything you say, boss." Bernie maneuvered the truck into the fast lane and made short order of the balance of their journey.

Ryan made a brief stop at Leslie's walk-in closet before entering the master suite on her mission of lust. There she let her eyes roam over shelf after shelf of Leslie's shoes. The awe and reverence many experienced in their places of worship Ryan felt in the presence of so many stylish, feminine shoes. Had her need not sprung from her deepest self with such pressing haste she would have lingered in that cell to appreciate the riches contained within. As it was she took her current favorite, a pair of grey snakeskin D'Orsay pumps, and turned for the bedroom.

A lone candle shone from the window seat. Its wavering light brought life to her sleeping mate's delicate features and golden hair. In sleep, as in wakefulness, Leslie was the essence of femininity. As with the shoes, Ryan couldn't take the time to explore her wide range of responses to her lover's enchanting femaleness.

Drunken, and in a pyretic state of sexual agitation, Ryan was only able to respond to a singular desire, the desire to conquer. No one had ever been more of a challenge to her than the woman lying before her now.

Heedless of the mid-September chill that could be felt even in their warm room, Ryan laid back the bedclothes to reveal Leslie's exquisite bronze-tanned form. She slipped the shoes on the naked feet with the greatest of care, pausing to stroke the now vital footwear with her trembling, rough hands.

This sexual prop had become an integral part of lovemaking for Ryan, so much so that she was rarely able to climax unless a pair of shoes were worn by her partner.

Her breath came whistling out as her excitement demanded that she leave off her admiration of her lover's stunningly clad feet to take immediate action. She willed her body into a steadiness that allowed her to act beyond the quaking lust that, at any moment, could erupt into uncontrollable frenzy.

As though begging for it, Leslie lay on her back with her legs well parted. Ryan's need to reduce this normally calm, aloof woman to a delirious bitch was almost more than she could bear.

Fully clothed in Levis, tailored shirt, leather jacket and boots — all in black — she mounted her wife and began to undulate her pelvis, digging it into the soft flesh beneath her with a fluid pace. She reveled in Leslie's soft helplessness momentarily before going on.

Seeking to arouse this urbane woman, she firmly placed her kisses in a hot line from the swell of Leslie's collarbone along the neck to her ear where she remained to allow her scorching breath to penetrate the dainty opening and the unaware slumber.

Leslie awakened in motion. Unconsciously her hips had begun an answer, rocking and swaying, to Ryan's plunging and stabbing. When she felt and heard the fiery breath filling her ear she moaned passionately, arching her neck. "Oh, Ryan. Ooan."

Ryan's voice was raspy. "You can't resist me. Can you, baby?"

"No, never," Leslie replied between long, low breaths. She

ran her hands upwards over Ryan's buttocks, then along her marvelous leather jacket. Its feel and musky aroma were the texture and smell of hard, dangerous living. There was a shadow of villainy that clung to Ryan. Against all reason Leslie found it exciting, even more when Ryan came to her drunk, demanding and on the verge of some kind of madness that Leslie couldn't fathom yet always responded to with her own brand of insanity.

"Night or day, asleep or awake, you know you can't turn away from me. You're *mine*," Ryan growled as she tightened her grip on Leslie's shoulders, driving her point home with a cruel thrust of her pubic bone into the wet cunt she so thoroughly owned.

"Oh, Ryan, take me," Leslie begged. "Take me hard!"

Unable to speak, Ryan groaned under the strain of her own need. She gripped her wife meanly and tore into her like a goat in rut, bucking her hips rapidly and panting loudly. Together they rode each other, uniting over and over at the site of their bodily appetites.

The time had never been when Ryan could climax as quickly as Leslie did when it was her first of the day. Sustained passion could only occur after that initial release. With no advance notice, Leslie broke open letting free her rapturous tensions and screams.

Ryan was easily strong enough to allow Leslie's fitful convulsions to go on, yet still maintain complete control over the situation and the woman in her grasp. Her assault continued unhindered in its quest for satisfaction. There was more to be had from this woman, and she was going to have it.

With furious, breathless urgency, Ryan urged her lover on. "I need you again, baby."

"Ooon. Yesss." Her moan of acceptance brought Ryan's mouth to hers. They joined, Ryan roughly kissing, Leslie wantonly meeting each kiss, each thrust, each probe of her capable tongue.

Electric waves stormed Leslie's body: waves caused by her lover's exaltation, unmatched prowess and ability to force Leslie to and beyond her limits. She melted to the demand, moaning and writhing, uncontrollably answering with more arousal, more surrender, more pleading.

Ryan was beside herself. She was conquering this woman, making her give it up and beg for more. It made her wild.

As Ryan's moans grew in intensity, Leslie took her cue to make her lover aware of the shoes she wore by digging the spikes of the heels into the back of Ryan's legs. The desired reaction was swift and sure. Ryan wailed loudly, "Yeah. Oh, god, baby. Ooohh," as she was swept under by her own orgasm. She stiffened and grimaced for several incoherent seconds, submerged as she was in her own ecstasy.

Scarcely recovered from the effects of her passion, she pulled herself off to one side of Leslie and plunged her fingers into her wife's sex cave. Furiously she pushed her partner to rise and peak, smiling smugly when Leslie screamed and thrashed about beyond control, the delirious bitch.

Satisfied and relieved in full, Ryan rested her head on Leslie's pillow and dozed off.

Smiling blissfully, Leslie memorized every glorious sensation: the intense relief, the damp skin, the divine lethargy, even the torture of being filled with the long, bony fingers of her sleeping lover. The digits had remained after they had done their duty — to tease, to conjure possibilities in her mind. Leslie had good reason to anticipate that the hand, sometimes having a will of its own, might induce a left-over orgasm or two. It had before.

The sweet agony of expectation lifted Leslie to the plateau of readiness. She closed her eyes and waited, frantically.

Then it happened. Ryan sighed and stirred, becoming partially aware. She loved these free orgasms. Suddenly she jiggled her fingers inside the moist, needy folds of Leslie's sex sending her over the edge yet one more time. The stillness of the night was punctuated with her feminine cry of gratification. Ryan savored the sound of it before she finally passed out. As she rolled over to her side of the bed, taking her fingers with her, she extracted another convulsion of pleasure from her wife.

At last, Leslie covered herself and returned to undisturbed sleep.

2

"Susan, welcome." Leslie extended her hands with a gesture of warm invitation. Her friend and one-time law partner was just the woman she needed to see right now. Instantly she felt her tension melt away at the sight of Susan Benson's cheerful face and happy smile. Someone at least, Leslie thought, has been spared in this dragnet of grief.

Susan took her friend's tenuous hands firmly in her own, drawing Leslie near. She took in the surroundings with a broad sweep of her eye noting that this campaign office, like all others of its kind, had a tasteless, but dynamic atmosphere about it — noisy, self-important, decked with streamers, slogans and unflattering blow-ups of the candidate — certainly nothing like the elegant woman in her grasp.

Leslie's ivory brown, lamb's wool dress, decorated with mallow pink beads splashed intricately over the bodice and up the sleeves from the wrist, fit snugly about her tallish form. Susan had never met anyone who could wear clothes the way Leslie did; she elevated it to an art form. Her full appreciation was inhibited only by the barest evidence around Leslie's halting grey eyes that this dear woman had been crying recently. No amount of stylish high fashion or expertly repaired make-up could hide that fact from Susan's educated gaze. She took command of the situation with ease.

"Hello, dear. Is there some place we may talk?" She followed Leslie into a small office away from the bustle in the main part of the Bennet Waterton for State House of Representatives campaign command post. This room was austere but private, and the only distraction was the blinking lights on the extension phone near the closed venetian blinds of the window.

Leslie closed the door behind them, and paced idly around the room. Susan quietly took a perch on the edge of the desk, watching for signposts.

Without warning, Leslie leveled her flashing, teasing eyes on Susan. "Come to spy on the enemy camp, have you?" But the humor was forced. She barely allowed Susan to reply in the negative before she continued, "It wouldn't matter anyway. Bennet is going to win."

The grim determination fueling Leslie's proclamation startled Susan. She didn't much care for Bennet Waterton. Although ably qualified for the post he was seeking, he was too ambitious for her taste. Susan was tired of ambitious people which was part of why she found Leslie and Ryan to be such refreshing company. While both were possessed of ticklish tempers, neither had vulgar aspirations in life. This was a side of Leslie she had never seen before. It worried her.

"No. As a matter of fact I've stopped having anything to do with 'the enemy'." Susan's voice was a little tighter than she wanted it to sound. It had been a difficult decision for her to choose between her friends. She wasn't accustomed to being placed in a position where she would *have* to. But seeing Leslie now, and knowing she was needed and would be appreciated, she was glad she had chosen in her favor. She found Leslie's puzzled expression endearing, and wanted to draw her into a hug, but couldn't.Susan had made it a point never to make the first move with this incredible woman. Her good crying shoulder was always available, but friendly hugs didn't pass between them for fear on Susan's part: fear that more would be born in her arms than she could handle. The desire was Susan's alone; Leslie had always thought of her as a solid, reliable friend, and right now a reliable friend was what was needed.

Susan chuckled when she thought about the scene she had just left. "You caused quite a stir over at the Delores Rhinehart for State House headquarters, my sly friend." Susan began to relax when she saw a whisper of satisfaction breathe over Leslie's beautiful face. So, *that's* what this is all about, Susan reassured herself.

She continued, knowing she had the blonde's full attention. "You know Del as well as I do so you can well imagine the expression on her face when her advance man read your name on the list of major supporters for Mr. Waterton's candidacy. I wish you had been there, Les, it was priceless. You'd have thought a judge had just given one of her clients the death penalty. When he told her how much money you'd contributed so far I thought she was going to swallow her tongue." Susan was not normally given to delight in another's discomfort but bringing light back into the room when Leslie smiled broadly, albeit viciously, warmed her heart. She almost felt guilty when she realized that she had taken direct pleasure from seeing how stunned *Dana* had looked when she heard the news. Leslie was positively beaming when Susan shared with her how Delores' vixen lover, Dana Shaeffer, had nearly fainted when she learned that Leslie was, almost single-handedly, financing Delores' opposition. It didn't take any special wit to see that Mr. Waterton had a decided edge since Leslie had her mate's everincreasing wealth at her disposal.

While Susan didn't know all the reasons, she knew enough to understand why Leslie was so motivated to have Delores lose the election, even to the point of crossing party lines to see to it. Less than a year had passed since Dana Shaeffer had succeeded in breaking the heart of their mutual friend, Brigid, driving her to temporary madness, and wreaking havoc in the O'Donnell household. Susan hadn't thought Leslie capable of revenge, but when she placed all the cards on the table in her mind she could see the justice of it. She even found herself approving.

Leslie interrupted her mental processes. "You paint a lovely picture, Susan. I'll be certain to have Delores' concession speech taped. But tell me why you're not having anything more to do with them. That doesn't sound like you."

Susan sighed heavily and shifted her weight on the edge of the desk. "Indeed, it doesn't. That's the part I wish no one had seen. Delores felt the need to blame somebody for all this and yours truly was drafted."

Leslie stepped closer and touched Susan's arm. It was seldom that Susan's clean, honest face was marred by displeasure. "Susan, she didn't," Leslie insisted. Of all people Delores could turn on, her law partner was anyone but the obvious choice.

She suspected the whipping post was intended to be Dana. It was no secret Delores wore blinders where her lover was concerned.

"She *did*." Susan was still smarting from the sting of Delores' mean assault on her character. After fifteen years of practice together, Susan never expected to be dismissed so . . . easily. Susan placed her hand over Leslie's for an electric moment, then patted it. "You did the right thing, quitting your practice, Les. Del has gotten worse since this thing with Dana and Brigid. If I didn't know better I'd almost think she suspected *me* of trying to make it with her little bitch of a wife."

Leslie gasped silently; she had never heard Susan speak ill of Dana before.

"Surprised? Don't be. I've never liked Dana. I like her even less now. But damn it, Les," Susan rose and paced a few steps, then turned to face her, "I've always been able to work things out with Del. Can you believe it? She actually told me to stop being your friend. Imagine. I was shocked. I don't care who wins this fucking election (excuse me), but I'm not going to bargain with my friends.

"I like you, Les. I like Ryan, and Brig. Hell, I do most of my work in the field anyway. I just go to that office out of habit. Del just invites me to her parties because I'm a hit with the ladies."

Both women had to laugh at that remark. Del knew how to mix women at her parties, and Susan was always a winner to have around. She would be missed and they both knew it.

"Leave it to Susan Benson to find the silver lining in every cloud," Leslie consoled. "You're always welcome in our company, Susan. I'm sorry to have come between you and Del. You've been friends for a long time." Leslie had mixed feelings about the news. Mostly she was relieved the falling-out hadn't gone the other way.

A silence moved in between them. Leslie found herself standing by the window lifting one of the slats in the blind. It was a meaningless move. Looking out the window did nothing to relieve her troubles; she wasn't even aware she was doing it.

Susan wanted to rescue her from her unseen burden. Unseen or no, she sensed this thing weighing upon her friend was more oppressive, more ruled by a powerful force she was no match for than she'd like to accept. Her protective instincts ran very high where Leslie was concerned. She was careful to not sound

18

judgmental when she asked softly, "How is Ryan these days?" It wasn't easy to keep a drinking problem hushed up in the circles Leslie and Susan traveled, still, it could be done. But Ryan was notorious for her hard drinking, and Leslie could be sensitive on that score.

"Well enough, I suppose," Leslie replied distractedly. Then she dropped the slat for emphasis and turned a pair of worried grey eyes toward Susan. "When she's sober." Leslie couldn't contrive to hide her pain any longer; Susan saw it and reacted to it instantly.

She tapped her shoulder indulgently, indicating it was as absorbent as ever. Leslie allowed herself to be enfolded into the warmth and comfort of Susan's solace. After a few moments she dried her eyes, sighing heavily.

"And when she isn't?" Susan pried gently.

"Phil has grounded her; she hasn't been flying for weeks."

Susan was relieved to hear that Ryan's mentor/father figure, Phil Peterson, kept the airborne public's best interests in mind by forcing Ryan to remain earthbound. She knew enough about Ryan to see the flight ban would cause problems on the home front. "Who's paying for that?" Susan hoped it wasn't Leslie.

"Sanji." Leslie's shoulders deflated, her head hung low. She was ashamed of Ryan's behavior toward their Jamaican charge. Sanji had entered into a totally submissive relationship with Ryan and Leslie; she was their complete responsibility. Leslie felt as though Sanji's trust in them had been betrayed.

"She abuses her horribly, Susan. I can't bear it. I've offered to support Sanji financially so she can move out, but she won't go. She acts like she expects Ryan to hurt her. She insists that she pledged to stand by Ryan no matter what, and will not budge from that stance." Leslie pulled away a little; Susan let her arm go slack.

"You have to admire her loyalty," Susan offered.

"Admiration expiates nothing," Leslie retorted.

"Who said it was your place to atone for Ryan's misuse of Sanji's masochism and devotion? Has she hit you?" Susan's concern mounted.

"No," Leslie reassured her quickly. "It's more like neglect." Her clarification was bitter. She, too, had pledged to stand by her mate, no matter what the cost. The expense was bleeding her emotional account dry.

"Neglect! Ryan? I've been around long enough to know a

woman like Ryan doesn't neglect someone she loves unless she's stopped loving her."

"That's not true. She neglected Dana for years but she loved her dearly," Leslie rationalized. She wished Ryan's neglect signified nothing, that Ryan still loved her, too.

Susan was discerning the truth although she didn't want to. The very possibility that Ryan might be in love with another woman was nearly beyond Susan's comprehension. The way she saw it, Ryan had for a lover the best woman she would ever find. How could she even *think* of another woman? Searching for the confirmation she prayed would not come, Susan stated, "She neglected Dana because she loved something else more." Susan took Leslie's upper arms into her grip to compel her friend to face her directly. "Or some*one* else." The fearful look on Leslie's face told her more than she wanted to know. "Leslie, no . . ." Susan breathed incredulously.

Leslie was frozen, speechless. When she blinked, tears played down her cheeks, unchecked.

"Oh, god." Susan gathered her friend into a firm embrace, holding her until there were no more tears.

Brigid tried to tell herself that she enjoyed these quiet late evening visits with Leslie, and occasionally managed to convince herself. More often, being 'friends' with her cousin's wife left her more frustrated than if she had stayed away. But despite herself and her better judgment, she came anyway—to sit, to watch, to be near this womanly vision sitting across from her now.

Brigid knew that if anyone discovered that a kitchen maid had been bribed to telephone her whenever Ryan left to go out drinking, the servant would be let go, but she had to take the chance. She had to be alone with Leslie, or as alone as Leslie would allow her to be, no matter what the risk.

It was no longer a question of what was right, or loyal, or fair to all involved. It was a matter of love, and Brigid had no more sense about her when she was in love than a March hare.

Night after night, she would call on Leslie, who would politely entertain her in the sitting room with pleasant conversation. All very proper. Brigid's invitations to Leslie to do otherwise were patently, but sweetly, refused.

Yet another fruitless evening was drawing to a close, leaving Brigid to cast about for ways to extend it. She picked her crutches up from the floor beside her and slipped her arms into the metal circles, grasping the padded grips tightly as if her fraying nerves could latch on and draw strength from their familiarity. She stood then, forcing herself to look away from the object of her unreasonable affection, moving toward the fireplace where she made a haphazard attempt to tend the fire in it.

Leslie closed her eyes briefly, gritting her teeth against her throbbing headache. A vibrating core of energy was drilling into the top of her skull with increasing urgency. She knew she was being summoned, her presence required elsewhere. She wished Brigid would leave without being asked to. To relax herself she fingered the waves of chestnut hair draped across her lap, bringing a slight nod of acknowledgement from the youth sitting at her feet, sewing.

When she opened her eyes again, Brigid was staring at her. Leslie marveled how her guest never let her missing leg keep her from standing proud and tall, six-foot tall. She had a well-balanced body—muscled hard and regular. Her strong, well-born looks—even red hair, sharp-lined bones, stern, narrow nose—were superfluous when set against her penetrating grey eyes.

Brigid looked away from Leslie. She didn't want to see a polite plea to leave play across the splendid face. Her eyes went everywhere but there—taking, one more time, a tour around the Victorian room. Somehow Leslie had managed to expunge the gloom normally present in the decor of that more gentle time. The sitting room was one of many miracles she had performed when she redecorated McKinley mansion. Brigid was pleased to have two of her own works of art, a ceramic floral arrangement and a portrait of her heart's fancy, mingled among the browns, greens and golds surrounding them.

When her gaze came to rest on Corelle, the young maid nestled into the folds of Leslie's pink silk lounging outfit, her heart snaked about itself and choked. Here was a girl, just turned twenty, who could be with Leslie as much as she pleased without causing a stir of jealousy or ill-will anywhere in the O'Donnell household. *She* would never be tactfully asked to leave, have *her* caresses carefully endured. No, she could just curl her voluptuous little body up in a ball at her Mistress' feet, lost in her needlework, and remain content in the knowledge that her service and devotion would never be thwarted. *Her* artwork — her ability to give without question — would never hang on the wall above the mantelpiece; it would cling gently and warmly to Leslie's perfect heart.

As if Leslie knew her darling handmaiden were under attack from her unwelcome guest, she leaned over to check the girl's progress with the tiny doily she was embroidering.

Brigid gasped.

Without realizing her folly, Leslie had unwittingly exasperated Brigid's already dangerous nervousness. Bending over had allowed her gown to fall open slightly at the top, exposing to Brigid's enlarged eyes her divine, conical-shaped breasts.

It was Corelle who noticed Brigid's determined approach and changed mood. She alerted her Mistress by squeezing her foot. Leslie sat up sharply, encountering the redhead's large hand as Brigid reached for her jaw to tip her head where she could look directly into her eyes.

Leslie did not like what she saw. That same look on Ryan would have melted her to a hot, liquid state of submission. On Brigid it spelled trouble. What had just been a headache before, was suddenly an overpowering, full-body pain.

Corelle and Leslie stood as one, bonding together to form the shield of feminine righteousness so effectively wielded by their foremothers for generations gone by. Leslie boosted her stance with her own abrupt need to quit this scene to go to a place where none could follow, where she was needed, and *immediately*.

"I must ask you to leave now, Brigid," Leslie demanded, breaking the noisy silence that had been woven between them for many long minutes.

"Please don't. Let me hold you." Brigid couldn't believe she had just spoken so openly of her need. Even less credible was what her arms seemed to be doing, independent of her control. She pulled Leslie close in an embrace that had no amount of friendship behind its intent, coming within a hair's breadth of kissing her full on the mouth, when Leslie's fingernails dug meanly into her ribs.

"*I said go*," Leslie ordered tersely through clenched teeth.

Brigid backed away instantly. She had never heard Leslie speak with such force and power before. Upon looking closely at the gentle woman, she knew she'd also never seen the faint greenish-white light shimmering about her body. For an instant, Brigid thought she heard a low-pitched hum coming from somewhere.

Once, when she was a teenager, she had happened upon her cousin, who had looked similarly. Brigid learned later that Ryan had been raising some kind of power. All Brigid knew was that she wanted no part of that or any other of Ryan's extraordinary abilities. If *Leslie* were going to start exhibiting these uncanny skills, then perhaps she *had* better move along.

Corelle handed her the large, sheepskin coat she had worn against the early snowstorm which had fallen the night before. Sensing the urgency of the moment, Brigid didn't stop to put it on before leaving. She tucked it under her arm, said good night and walked quickly toward the main hall on her way out of the great mansion.

Brigid's departure sparked a flurry of activity in Leslie. She called Sanji's name sharply, then went to the small writing desk near the window. She wrote a short note, sealed it, handed it to the stunning black woman who had just appeared at her side.

"Give this to your Master when she returns," she commanded, breaking the formal silence between them. She called out to the two younger women on her way to her office, "I am to be disturbed by *no* one, for any reason." She didn't wait for confirmation; she knew for certainty that her orders would be obeyed to the letter. The door to her office was closed impatiently behind her, blocking out the physical world with all its distractions and troubles.

Sanji smiled at the bewildered look on Corelle's face. While each of them were considered sex-slaves in the O'Donnell household, Sanji had what could only be termed seniority, and it was her who Corelle had learned to consult at a time like this.

In a mild sort of way, Sanji had grown attached to this frail, vulnerable morsel of womanhood. In secret, she had taken advantage of Corelle's position as a subordinate slave—many times. Some of the violence she suffered at the hands of her Master, Ryan, tumbled down the pecking order to intimidate Leslie's prized possession, the little Irish immigrant, Corelle.

Sanji knew Corelle was too frightened of her to tell anyone of the abuse, sexual and physical, she inflicted upon her. Neglect being a byword at McKinley, Sanji had begun to suspect that Corelle had learned to like the furtive pinching, tweaking and being caught in out of the way places like wine cellars where she had to submit to having her abundant breasts mashed and always ready sex ploughed by long, black fingers.

It was all so simple for Sanji to take her frustrations out on the innocent servant; there wasn't even any worry about leaving bruises on her fertile little body. If Leslie discovered them, she mistook them for ones left by Ryan; if Ryan noticed them (which she never did), she would attribute them to her own drunken rages. Corelle was never the object of such rages, but she had been caught in the cross-fire a time or two.

But there was also a tender place in Sanji's heart for Corelle. The girl was *so* innocent, and in a world where such guileless-ness was virtually non-existent, Sanji couldn't help feeling pro-tective toward her sister slave.

She patted Corelle on the head then let her hand travel down to Corelle's right, and larger, breast. "Go to bed, now, little one." Sanji allowed her tactile senses to revel in the feel of Corelle's linen batiste uniform, under which she knew was a pastel blue lace chemise that would lift so easily . . . "Everything will be just fine here. Your Lady is well but will be gone for a time," Sanji reassured while massaging the thimble-like tip of the toy in her grasp. She explained that, once again, their Mis-tress was being called away — to an out-of-body condition — but would return unharmed and refreshed. This Sanji knew instinc-tively when she saw the familiar shroud of light enveloping Leslie, the same as had circled Ryan in the past.

She pulled and twisted the cloth and nipple just long enough to make Corelle want more. She wanted to see the pliant, plead-ing look on that round face before she dismissed her for the night . . . a night of frustration and longing since neither of them were allowed to touch themselves. But Sanji knew in her heart that tonight she wouldn't have to worry about her own satisfaction. Tonight she would have Ryan to herself or die trying. One last tweak yielded a tiny whimper, and she sent Corelle on her way.

Sanji didn't have long to wait for Ryan's return. The fre-quently absent, often drunk, lord and Master of McKinley arrived earlier than usual and under her own power. Sanji's heart pounded in time with the sound of the solid footsteps as

24

Ryan made her way to the south wing of the mansion where Leslie's office was situated.

The glow of lights from that quarter led the way for Ryan who would have normally turned toward the master suite on a night like this one. Her lust no less dampened by the knowledge that her exquisite wife was still awake, Ryan was surprised to see Leslie's door closed, and Sanji on sentry duty outside it. She slowed her pace, then came to a full, nervous halt next to her alluring slave.

Sanji was quick to hand the sealed note to Ryan, heading her off before she could open the door that barred her way to her wife. She had read Ryan's mood even before she caught sight of her, and was assured that all she need do was make herself available and provocative to get her way with this tyrant. Too easy.

"My Lady asked that I give this to you, Master." Sanji held back her premature smile of victory. Instead she stepped a finger's width closer, assuming an appealing pose and willing her womanly fragrance to drift into reach of Ryan's highly attuned sensory field. Her voice was careful, obedient, smooth. She knew how to influence this black-clad despot.

Ryan took the clean, silver-grey note, broke the seal, and read it with interest: My Darling (the even script read) I have been called away so cannot be here to welcome you when you arrive. I shall miss you, and pray that my return is swift. Your Dove.

Gazing thoughtfully into space, Ryan tapped the note on her palm three sharp times as she correctly surmised where her wife might be, and why. To reassure herself that all was well, she gently opened the door before her to peer inside the darkened room. The faint greenish light had increased noticeably, clinging in a vibrant cylinder about Leslie's body. Ryan nodded her acceptance, closing the door quietly.

A blink of an eye later, Ryan turned to notice the woman standing beside her. The slow, wicked smile of approval showed Sanji everything she wanted to see — she had captured the interest of the most virile, passionate, demanding woman she had ever known. Again. These coy, fiery, dangerous games they played together were what Sanji longed for more than life itself. This knee-weakening lust they experienced for each other was limited only by the boundaries of the physical world — there was nothing they wouldn't do to keep the flow of passion unabated.

Ryan took it *all* in. Again. The mass of wiry hair that she knew would fill her vicious grip before the night was out; the dusky eyes of soot she would fall in and out of a dozen times before she would know any measure of fulfillment; the long, flexible neck she would strain to its limits; the marvelous, seal-colored skin that would set itself against her ghostly paleness to weave a spell of enchantment and abandon that would carry them both beyond the normal range of experience. And how this witch could drape garments about her five foot, eight package of beauty. Breathtaking.

Ryan was glad to see the coppery, velvet cape hugging Sanji's shoulders; it meant that what was beneath it was backless. Ryan loved backless dresses. The cape was for everyone else's benefit. Ryan felt nothing but pride when she viewed the ruinous scars on her slave's back. They were a permanent symbol of Sanji's unfailing devotion. For even after having been severely punished for a now-forgotten wrong, Sanji remained to serve. And would continue to do so — forever.

Ryan unfastened the catch at the throat of the knee-length wrap, then pushed it over the magnificent shoulders of its wearer.

And the game began.

"Hsss." Ryan's breathy hiss skimmed coldly over her teeth to make way for the hot moan that made the return trip.

Revealed before her was a slip of a dress fashioned completely from iridescent copper bugle beads: no fabric, no seams, no zippers. In fact, the imagination needed to get up and stretch to call it a proper dress, for the woven beadwork was barely long enough to cover Sanji's charcoal sex, only just tickling her sensitive backside. The visual effect that seared through Ryan like lasers was that the whole, somewhat heavy garment was suspended entirely from the white gold rings which passed through Sanji's pierced nipples.

Ryan stared for a goodly long time, shifting the control Sanji had procured through the stealth of her brazenness back to where it belonged: with the Master. She casually lit a cigarette, letting her knowing gaze bore into her slave's global breasts.

Sanji, for all her bold, haughty rebelliousness, had yet to find a way to restrain her reaction to Ryan's pitiless evaluation. She squirmed. She was meant to. A woman didn't live who wouldn't become embarassingly aware of her own need and motives when subjected to Ryan's imperious, all-consuming appraisal.

When Sanji shifted her body, the beads of her dress made a crackling noise as their weight swayed with her motion, tugging on her now alert, midnight nipples. Now all attention, hers and Ryan's, were focused on her straining teats; they were hard and proud, proud to bear their burden, She had worn the tantalizing thing several nights in a row never knowing when, if ever, she would be in a position to waylay her Master. In that time she had grown not only accustomed, but addicted to the pleasurable pain concentrated in her ultra-sensitive nipples. Every step she took served to remind her of her desire, her need.

And now, melting under Ryan's gaze, she was humiliated by the extent of her need. Her body flowed and vibrated; her breathing deepened. The entire universe began and ended on her black nubs.

"You wench," Ryan taunted, "There's no limit to your whorish methods. I ought to take you to the bar like that . . . let everyone watch these beads," Ryan fondled the fringe dangling below Sanji's moist sex, "tug and sway from your tits."

"Oh, Master," Sanji nearly wept from the excitement of Ryan's touch and suggestion. She wanted, but was afraid of, what she was proposing. The very vivid memory of when Ryan *had* made her a public sex object at one of the bars pulled the strength from her knees, buckling them, and making her fall into Ryan's very willing arms.

The chill of Ryan's leather jacket on her breasts combined with the burning fingers digging into her ample buttocks, weakening her. Her moans scored Ryan's nerves with razors of need. Except that they risked disturbing Leslie on her delicate journey, the impassioned couple would have fallen to the floor, lost in the blackness of their gluttony.

It was Ryan who exercised more control than she thought she could summon to drag Sanji away and up to her slave quarters. The dress noisily hastened along with them, sending shots of pain through Sanji's receptive body. Ryan would have liked to have watched the effect, but she knew better. Time was of the essence.

In the bitterly stark white room, Ryan turned on her slave, forcing her to her knees with one hard thrust downward. Sanji, a dancer by training, accomplished her hard fall with graceful, mindless action. In her condition she was pliable to the point of sacrifice. Ryan forced her buttocks back on her heels, then straddled the sweating, panting face, pulling Sanji backwards to a position where she had absolutely no balance. Her head had no support save the clawing grasp of her Master's ungovernable need. Ryan tangled her fingers into Sanji's mass of soft hair and *yanked* her extraordinary mouth into her own flammable sex.

"Huuuh . . . god . . . bitch," Ryan exclaimed. This was freedom — abandonment at its height. Ryan mashed and jabbed her sex into Sanji's face with a force that could only be sustained by unleashed passion and total disregard for suffering. She single-mindedly took her own pleasure, pushing back and forth over Sanji's luscious lips.

"Take it! Take it, baby." Ryan was out of her mind with the thrill of forcing her slave to withstand so much pain and abuse while giving so much pleasure.

And Sanji took it. All of it. She bore up under the constant and electric pain. When in this position, the only place she had ever been allowed to place her hands was limply on the spikes of her heels. There, they would make her aware of her feminine vulnerability, rob her of the support she might otherwise gain from bracing them on the floor below her shoulders, or break her impending fall.

Ryan was climbing that wall of lust she would fling herself headlong from into the darkness beyond. Her ascent was rapid and loud. Her moans grew in intensity and then . . . "Oh, goohhnnd!" Waves, contractions, release, the snapping of sanity, the ignition of blue and white fire singed every nerve, cell and atom of Ryan's body.

She dropped Sanji's head, and flung her hands against the cold wall in front of her. "Oh, fuck, Sanji," she panted. Her arms were locked to brace her satisfied, weakening body.

Sanji took it all in with glowing pride. Her body was folded back on itself, her head was nestled between Ryan's tailored boots. The sight above her never ceased to gratify her. This hardened, mean taskmaster — long-legged, trim, dressed for danger — panting and heaving, reduced, and trying to recover from her own passion. Passion that fed on itself, and thrived on its own need to perpetuate itself, over and over again, through Sanji's willing submission. It was at times like these that Sanji worshipped her Master in every way, in every detail.

When Ryan regained her strength, she picked her slave off the floor, placed her on her back on the bed and climbed atop her. With little effort on either woman's part, Ryan soared near her sexual zenith a second time. On this trip she had with her her hungry partner. This dark sex goddess matched her hammering with sliding, grinding and pulsing. Ryan's weight ground the beadwork into Sanji's damp skin, but never so cruelly as where the Master's denim-bound bone ground into the slave's tortured pubis.

Senselessly each robbed the other of her predatory lust. The exchange was made amidst wild grapplings, kisses and cries of relief.

Sanji cared nothing for what religious people called a heaven in the after-life; she had found all that could comprise her image of heaven in her mortal, clinging arms. It wasn't so dark in her slave quarters that she couldn't make out every minute detail of satisfaction on her Master's pale face. In a room purposely kept free of distractions, she could hear each ragged breath of contentment, taste the bittersweet whiskey and cigarettes left from Ryan's ravaging kisses, feel the diminishing heartbeats in their heaving breasts, smell their womanly sweat.

Sanji enjoyed lying still beneath this unpredictable, satyric virago. Doing so allowed her time to memorize each sensation, and enable Ryan to unwind enough to determine if she wanted more from her nymphomaniac slave. Sanji was *always* ready to give more, even if she couldn't make her muscles obey her any longer, if she lost her voice from screaming, if she were feeling the kind of *real* pain that no sexual arousal could mask any longer. Whatever Ryan required of her, she would give. And had given in the past.

But Ryan's thoughts had traveled a different road. What she wanted from Sanji now would be easy for the concubine to give. Ryan brought her lips close to Sanji's soft ear, lingered there while her desire mounted, they paved each word with graveled authority. "I'm going to lick your *pussy*, bitch."

A shudder of excitement traveled Sanji's length. Her moan was deep and tearful; it had been many months since her Master had bestowed such an honor upon her. The perfect slave that she was, she was grateful. "Thank you, Master," came her stage whisper. Then again, even more genuinely, "Thank you."

On her way to her prize, Ryan stopped to comment on the decoration Sanji had created for her body. "This is beautiful!" she admired.

Once between Sanji's talented legs, Ryan wasted no time

parting her sensitive sex lips, and gorging herself on the sweet woman-need of Sanji's cunt.

The only thing that could make Sanji's pleasure more intense was what Ryan was doing to her nipples by tugging on the fringe of her dress in time with the hard, merciless thrusts of the gifted tongue into her open crevice of craving.

Sanji was quite comfortable in the animalistic state of non-thinking, non-reasoning excess. She had no inhibitions about letting her mind loose to revel in every millisecond of searing pleasure Ryan created for her by taking her hard and long, fast and deep, stroke after stroke, thrust after thrust. She could completely let go, knowing full well that Ryan was a tireless cunnilinguist; that this gourmet's palate at times ran to the cruder, more robust tastes.

Years ago a tacit promise had been made to her that she would never be left unsatisfied in this act, that she could have as much as she wished and more than she could bear without end until she herself set the limits by falling over the knife edge of her own stamina and need.

Words did not exist for what Sanji felt next. Only those who have traveled to that frightening world of utter incontinence can name it. The rest may only hope to skirt the edges of such intoxication and freedom. Ryan and Sanji were frequent visitors to that land of no name, enough so that they had discovered many new ways to call it — mostly it sounded like screams and sighs and fear and happiness.

Their return to general awareness was as reluctant as it was inevitable. Ryan would sleep with Sanji on this night, satisfied, wrapped around her blissful body, and they would know contentment.

3

Leslie closed her eyes, pulled her breathing down to a shallow maintenance level, blanked out all conscious thought, and let her inner self guide her to the Council chambers from whence she was being so painfully summoned.

Her journey was accomplished safely, as she knew it would be. Her last visit to the spirit world some months before had been to witness her lover, Ryan, transform into her true self, Blaise, only to rekindle the bond of love with the wicked demi-goddess, Anara. It had been the most painful event she had ever endured in her eons of existence.

To protect herself from further shock, Leslie had seen fit to return from her previous spirit excursion with full knowledge of who she was and what she was about. She had known this summons from her Council would be forthcoming, and was prepared for it.

In the misty antechamber of the Council room, she stood quietly, calming herself, suppressing the urge to pace. Let them wait, she instructed herself. She was certain that her attendance was known to the others inside the vaulted chamber. A show of power was necessary here. They must not think me unwilling to leave my earthly state, however briefly, or reluctant to officiate these proceedings, the gentle Queen reminded herself.

Once she felt whole and in control, she nodded to the young

servant who had been watching her with a mixture of fear and admiration. The youth stole away behind a heavy, brown curtain to tell the court herald that the Queen was ready to make her entrance.

The Queen took a deep breath as she listened to the last of the announcement.

". . . graces us with her presence. The Veiled One, Her Sovereign Queen Regent of the Throne of Council, The One Who Seeks Knowledge and Justice," the bold-voiced crier let the last word resonate throughout the chamber with an air of supreme importance, signaling The One Who Seeks Knowledge and Justice to part the curtains, and glide into the brilliantly lighted chambers of Council.

The Queen—whose real name (the name the herald did not know and could not utter) was Venadia—moved gracefully up the steps to her gilded throne. Under her gauzy Veils she was smiling. It never ceased to amuse her when she heard the hisses and murmurs of awe that traveled along and back the length of the great table whenever she entered the Council room.

Her appearances in Council were as infrequent as they were short, never allowing any of the six members to become too familiar with her or accustomed to her mien. None of the six had ever learned her true name or had viewed her countenance without her Veils. She was the image of mystery. She preferred to keep it that way.

Venadia silently took her seat and turned her unseen gaze on the lot of them. Even now none of them had erased the look of fascination on their various faces.

Venadia surveyed each one thoughtfully.

Ramonye: worthy of his position on Council. His forest green velvet robes were draped elegantly about him making him so appealing, even to her. Consort to ancient goddesses gone by, he embodied all that was refined and graceful. He managed his court intrigues and betrayals with finesse and perfect manners. Venadia didn't trust him one iota. He could be counted on, in the struggle to come, only for that which would elevate his position or bring him closer to whatever female he sought to find him attractive. And these days that female was Anara, the Contender for Venadia's soon to be vacated Throne.

Bilouge: a creature whose company Venadia could not abide. Nonetheless this gynandros persona could be trusted and relied upon if it saw the right of a matter. Venadia suspected the feather-bedecked courtier was within the boundaries of her camp.

The next two Council members, The Goddess of Light and Caspia, were most definitely enemies. Their outspoken support for Anara to become the next Queen Regent of The Throne of Council was a sour echo in the back of Venadia's mind. Venadia let her gaze linger on the dangerous Goddess of Light. Her own smile long since faded, Venadia studied the birth of a devious grin in the corners of the Goddess' mouth. This deity didn't allow herself to be overcome by her own unsettling fear of Venadia the way the others did. She could conquer hers, and was doing so before the Queen's very eyes.

The Goddess of Light knew better than any that beneath their leader's placid veneer was a menacing foe when aroused. Despite her show of courage, the Goddess of Light was more afraid of Venadia's unseen power than anyone.

Venadia made a mental note: She remembers my admonition, and has not flooded this primordial meeting place with her blinding light. She's very beautiful when she behaves, Venadia added, taking in the almost solemn appearance of the Goddess' ball-like, liquid state.

Caspia rated only a cursory glance. The perfect foil for the peaceful Queen, this earth-colored warrioress was as restless as Venadia was sedate. No labor of thought was needed to determine that it had been this great fighter who had called forth the Council. Caspia was itching for the battle to begin. She always was. Either opponent, Anara or Blaise, was far more to her liking that this hauntingly ethereal, imperturable rival she'd had to deal with for far too long.

The remaining two, Pliquay and Serdon, were firm supporters of Venadia and all she had tried to accomplish during her reign. Overseers of creativity and life, these two women, beauties in their own right, were lovers much the same as Venadia and Blaise had been—forever. They were deeply saddened by the unhappy circumstances Venadia now faced.

It was Serdon—round, bluish-black face sparkling in the brightness surrounding her—who broached the subject of their meeting. "My Queen, it has been agreed that we must discuss the matter of the Contender taking her opponent for The Throne as a consort." Serdon's voice was soft and melodic, her bearing respectful and compassionate. The very thought that her lovely mate, Pliquay, might do as Blaise had done by taking another to her side made Serdon shudder. She was astounded by how steady her leader was under the circumstances.

Whispers of assent skimmed the now tense surface of emotions filling the room. Serdon moved her eyes quickly about. There wasn't one among them who hadn't taken a turn in a bed other than hers or his own, but none here who was mated for eternity to another had ever cast aside her dearest one for someone else. This was a serious infraction, made even more so by the unseemliness of rightful *enemies* defying such precedent.

Serdon let her eyes rise carefully to The Throne and her wondrous Queen. The delicacy of Venadia's ivory Veils, the filamentary gold hems, the barest evidence of black-diamond neck scalloping flowed together to take the viewer off guard, and keep her there. It was not possible to look at a Veiled Venadia and form a solid image of what she looked like. Serdon's eyesight was keener than most; what she could not see, she could intuit, but there was sadness under those Veils — deep, heartbroken sadness. The giver of life took back her eyes, but not her determination to see this matter resolved.

"They can't and won't do battle if they are lovers!" Caspia stormed, slamming her fist on the ancient table with a force that rocked it.

Everyone, including Venadia, ignored the outburst; they were accustomed to Caspia's impatient, aggressive ways.

"Caspia has a point, my Queen," Ramonye offered smoothly. "This liaison between Anara and Blaise must cease. They know the rules."

Venadia settled her stomach with a practiced mental effort. To be called "My Queen" by Ramonye was a bit much. It could have been accepted as a show of respect were he not given to using that same address with Anara — someone Venadia loathed. But worse were his obvious motives for wanting to see this relationship between Blaise and his prey, Anara, end. He had designs on sharing The Throne with Anara (so sure he was that she would defeat Blaise), and his chances were diminished greatly by Anara's restoration of Blaise as her consort.

"Truly, Sovereign Queen," Pliquay spoke firmly and swiftly, "it was quite enough that they had been lovers in a physical embodiment, but for them to continue this nonsense in the spirit is out of the question. We cannot let this go on."

Venadia let her eyes rest searchingly on her friend. Of all her Council members, this comely demi-goddess with skin the color of goldenrods, was the one she would have believed to be the most understanding of Blaise and Anara's rediscovered love.

"Indeed!" chirped the flippant, nervous Bilouge. "It's got to stop."

Venadia suppressed a laugh. As irritating as Bilouge could be, there was never any lack of humor there, intentional or otherwise. She simply could not take it seriously.

Venadia let them vent their frustrations for a while longer, all the time watching the Goddess of Light who remained silent. This is ridiculous, Venadia mused. She must know how suspicious it seems for her to refrain from acting as foolishly as the others. Perhaps she knows there is nothing I can do about Blaise and Anara. She settled in her Throne and sighed, drawing all attention to herself, as she had meant to do.

Suddenly, all present became embarrassingly aware that their Queen hadn't spoken a word since her arrival. All eyes were on her.

When Venadia spoke, her voice was clear and forceful. "I have searched the records for any indication that this may have happened in the past." She kept her speech even, leaving no room for interruption or dissent. "Certainly, it has been tried. The thought that opponents avoiding battle by co-ruling The Throne might be illegal is simply that: a thought. One perpetuated time out of mind by members of Council who did not wish to serve a dual-purposed administration. In no place or at any time has it been specifically mandated that this cannot be so."

"Well, I think it should be!" Caspia erupted, springing from her seat.

Despite her fervent desire not to, Venadia found she had to address her aggressor. "The Laws of the Universe are set, *Caspia*, and with reason. This Council was not called to debate the wisdom of our predecessors." Caspia slowly took her seat, scorned into silence. She accepted her humiliation and chastisement with a pride known well of warrioresses.

The Goddess of Light shifted nervously in her seat. She had hoped that Venadia would have shown an inkling of weakness, something that would have left her vulnerable to a subtle attack, or a tiring filibuster at the very least. But no, Venadia had been as wise, patient and serene as ever. It looked as though her record of making short order of Council meetings would stay intact to the last. The other members looked at one another or their laps like scolded children.

Venadia rose. "Blaise and Anara must resolve this struggle in their own way. *We* must wait until the final outcome, and abide by it, however unpalatable it may be." Venadia condescended to tag the last phrase on to let her Council know she was no more pleased about this love affair than they were. With that parting comment, she nodded to the herald to announce her departure.

Each Council member rose solemnly in respect. All were lost in their own thoughts as their Sovereign Queen took quiet leave of their company.

Venadia wasn't sure why she'd come to this oasis; it just seemed like the thing to do. She felt relaxed there among the crystals and incense. No, that isn't why I'm here, she corrected herself. Face it, Venadia, you *want* to see her. What the Queen wouldn't go on to tell herself was that she was lonely, she missed Blaise, her heart was broken, and she was sick and tired of feeling the way she did — lost, and alone.

She had never felt like this before. Blaise, in all her images and growth processes, had always been there whenever Venadia needed her. Venadia had always been there for Blaise as well. Always. Suddenly, Venadia did something else she hadn't done, at least not in the last several millinneums: she cried.

Then the area around her became warm, growing hotter and hotter, drying her tears. Yes, this was who she needed to see.

The Goddess of Fire brought together her configuration of white-hot qualities, shaping herself into a tangible form Venadia would appreciate. She took the weeping Queen into her vibrant arms, and held her close. They stayed in this wordless mesh of comfort for a time before greeting one another.

'Hestia, welcome. Your warmth gladdens my heart." Venadia and the Goddess were the closest of friends, and easy with allowing the use of her name of power by the other.

"Venadia, your sorrow breaks mine. If I can be even a small solace, I am honored." Hestia's powerful, hollow voice resonated the crystals around them, making them hum gently and soothingly.

Venadia gazed into her friend's mutable, flamelike eyes. The gesture had just the hint of invitation Hestia was waiting for. She slowly lifted the layers of Veils to reveal the unmatched beauty of Venadia's ivory porcelain features, her golden eyes, glass-clear hair and sensuous lips a color of yellow known only to a few beings who lived beyond the realm of the physical world and its limitations of the imagination.

Hestia patently ignored the black diamond scalloping along the neckline of Venadia's shift. That decoration represented the undying love Venadia was supposed to share for all eternity with Blaise. A love gone now — or so Hestia was more than willing to believe. Her own smoldering love for this radiant eyeful was known to both sovereigns, and had been there longer than either of them could remember.

This, at last, was the time Hestia had waited for. Her passion skirted the edges of her form with flares of need. The show of need mesmerized and enticed the vulnerable Queen. Indeed, now. Take advantage of her, Hestia, the Goddess encouraged herself. This is her one weakness, fire. Give it to her, she craves it.

And Venadia did crave it — with every fibre of her soul. The need Blaise normally filled was left gaping open, wide, unprotected.

When their lips touched, Venadia went limp, dragging Hestia into the cavern of her want. Hestia fell willingly. Her desire filled every cave and hall of Venadia's empty heart.

Not strangely, Venadia was everything Hestia hoped for, and more. She had known other lovers who had demanded patience on her part (imagine fire being patient), and she had always found a way to contain her devouring passion. Venadia made no such demand on her. She was ready to be consumed, and for that the Goddess mentally thanked Blaise. Venadia, finally, had learned abandon.

There might be other times when Venadia would submit to her appetite, but Hestia wasn't willing to take that chance. She was going to make certain that Venadia took everything she had to give that had been stored up for so long a time.

Surrounding the two of them was an impenetrable wall of fiery Veils which assured them all the privacy they required to carry on with surrender. With sleight of hand ease, Hestia removed layer upon layer of Venadia's sheer Veils until there was only one left. This she would wait to remove, she had *some* patience. And the delicate undershift, while doing nothing to disguise Venadia's exquisite body, did everything to highlight her curves and shadows, tips and burrows.

Venadia was in a state of complete vulnerability. Thrilling

waves of excitement chased about inside her as she lay before the Goddess of Fire—hypnotically waiting for, tautly anticipating the first searing touch of Hestia's scorching hand. Her body gave off every conceivable message to indicate precisely *where* she wanted that touch to be.

Hestia smiled and thought: Venadia the forbearing, Venadia the stoic . . . how deliciously easy it was to make her Venadia the breathless, Venadia the fretful.

But Hestia's itch was desperately in need of scratching, too. Venadia couldn't want to be burned any more than Hestia wanted to burn her.

Slowly, she extended her flaming hand, reaching for the utterly divine café au lait nipple on Venadia's left breast. It stood erect, making a tent of the gossamer fabric shielding it. The breast itself was round and heavy, rising and falling more and more rapidly as Venadia's breathing grew in expectation.

The ages of suspense between these two intimates came to a much longed for end when Hestia firmly grasped Venadia's unreluctant breast.

Venadia's lips parted as her face registered a brief moment of surprise. She took a *long, deep* breath which she held for what seemed like a gratifying forever to both women; her eyes closed partially as her expression took on every nuance of bliss.

The Veil and flesh were left unscathed. This burning took place far down inside Venadia's inner soul. Her neck muscles went limp and her head melted backwards as she began to let her breath seep out in a luxurious sigh. "Ohh, yesss," came her complete assent.

Hestia took the mound of flesh in her avaricious clutch and bore into its softness with fingers made to seek and penetrate, sear and purge.

Venadia wanted to be taken greedily, and soon. She wound her slender fingers through her Goddess' scintillating mass of hair, encircled the nape of her neck, and brought her head down . . . to her other breast . . . which begged to be sucked, and bitten, and teased.

One has not heard the truest sound of delight until one has been privy to the moans of desire of a Goddess. There is simply no sound to compare to it. Indeed, the sound would drive mortal women mad.

Venadia was equal to the utterings of her deified lover. Between Hestia's vocal surges and Venadia's full screams, crystals (among them some of the first ever made) began to shatter about them.

Spurred on by her urgent need to have all this Queen had to offer, Hestia's blazing hand lifted the last ivory-colored Veil above her quarry's breasts then, quickly and almost hurtfully, spread Venadia's legs wide. The eye of her recall guided her fingers past the transparent sex hair to the sacred place within. Sacred or no, this was a time for debauchery. Venadia's sex, for all its virginal appearance, was ready and eager to accept this scalding ravaging.

Hestia opened the flower and gutted it.

"HESTIA!!!" Venadia wailed. Her pelvis rocked and lifted into the attack. Hestia thrust an ivory thigh between her incandescent ones, and rode her feminine mount furiously, all the while bruising the breast in her mouth with impunity.

When these two divinities consummated their all-powerful passion for one another, all that was left were the ashes of their need. They had taken the white, pure and perfect lust, bathed in it, exchanged their souls for it for a millisecond flash, then landed softly into steamy clouds of satisfaction and keen pleasure.

Hestia's spectacular display of leaping flames calmed to a warm, ember-like roll of heat. She was completely sated and restored. This was an experience she would not soon forget, and would wish to repeat again. Venadia's willingness had taken her by surprise; she had no idea the Queen was so capable of sustaining such unhindered ability to tolerate the essence of her element. An unusual skill indeed.

Venadia was pleased, relaxed, renewed. This was precisely the tonic she needed to go on, to endure what lay ahead of her. It was she who finally pulled away from their tender embrace, mindful of what was certain to be a by-product of their deepened intimacy: Hestia's desire to deepen it further still. She smoothed her light shift over her skin, and began to dress.

Hestia took her hand suddenly, unwilling to let the precious moment pass. "Linger, my sweet." They both knew that Venadia's physical body did not yet require her return, there was still time.

Venadia turned to look into the entreatingly soft eyes of her Goddess friend. Their invitation grew more seductive as the waiting passed between them, each knowing that what Hestia was hoping would come to pass, wouldn't. It was Hestia's fervent wish that this ivory beauty would find she needed more than just this temporary comfort; Venadia prayed selfishly that this embodiment of flames would always be there for her without requiring a commitment she wasn't willing to make.

"The temptation is strong, Hestia. You have been very good to me . . ."

Hestia pulled the Queen down into her arms, and kissed her with awakening need.

"Don't," Venadia managed to implore as she withdrew, setting herself with determination. "It is difficult enough, Hestia. Do not prey upon my weakness or my unbeloved lot."

Hestia settled herself in the face of Venadia's stern words. No one knew better how true they were than she herself did. She *was* trying to take advantage of Venadia. She could succeed, too, but didn't want love won in that fashion. In addition, Venadia didn't need to hear any more about the tragedy of her loss. Hestia saw no point in undoing the good the sad Queen gained from their tryst. "I shall miss you, dearest," the Goddess said quietly in compliance with her friend's wishes. She watched as Venadia dressed again, then stood before her calmly.

"I don't know how to thank you properly for sharing yourself with me. I know you want more," Venadia added cautiously.

"One last kiss before you go?" the Goddess requested.

The Queen smiled. "Yes," she agreed pleasantly.

Hestia lifted the Veils once more, gazed upon the radiant, peaceful face, and whispered a prayer of gratefulness, then: "I shall love you always, Venadia. Remember that, and that I am here . . . whenever you may need me." The kiss was gentle, filled with caring, and not long enough to suit the Goddess. She replaced the Veils, granted her friend a safe journey, and disappeared.

Venadia left silently.

When Leslie became aware of her breathing the house was quiet, everyone was asleep. She felt refreshed, tranquil. In that state her attention was drawn to her hand. She opened it, and saw an object, felt its power, caught a glint of moonlight reflecting from it. Curious to the last, Leslie stood and walked over to the window nearest the connected greenhouse to hold the piece up to the incoming glow. She smiled serenely. In her palm was a broken fragment of ancient crystal, hard and glistening, to remind her that the way back was hers for the traveling.

"Oh, my," Leslie exclaimed with a start. She had just stepped indoors after a lengthy exchange with the head gardener about the fall planting schedule, and was surprised to find Sanji sprawled at her feet.

The young black woman was equally startled to encounter her Mistress. Only once before had Leslie witnessed one of Ryan's violent outrages where *Sanji* was the object; she had been horrified and unable to act in the slave's behalf.

Leslie bent over and helped her sit up while she inspected the damage with one swift glance before turning her hardened gaze on the perpetrator: she saw a bleeding cut on Sanji's face from the barb of a whip, an impression left from the blow that had dashed this helpless bondmaid to the floor; her pretty gown ripped from her right side exposing her breast which was also scored with weals, some bleeding, others nearly. Nothing that wouldn't heal easily, but Leslie sensed that this battle hadn't heated up to its full fury yet. Sanji's continued health wasn't assured on any count.

Leslie straightened and whirled around to face Ryan who was standing dangerously close. What she saw chilled her heart.

Ryan's feet were spread firmly apart, her arms folded across her leather-covered chest. The stout handled, three-tailed whip was in keeping with the overall theme of black, and was held purposefully in her translucent hand. The tails dangled menacingly, drawing the eye again and again to their threat. The whip was a restful sight in comparison to what flared from Ryan's angry, jade eyes.

Leslie stepped between her lover and her vassal, summoning every scrap of courage to champion Sanji. "That's enough, Ryan. Leave her alone." Her delivery was deliberate, but there was an undercurrent of wariness on her side of the battleline. Ryan's temper was chancy at best; she was taking a frightening gamble that something sane would grip her mate and defuse the situation.

Leslie was banking that that something was Ryan's respect for her. Even in her most destructive episodes, Ryan couldn't lift a hand against this special woman. Leslie hoped that, although Ryan seemed unable to keep from hurting her emotionally, she couldn't and wouldn't hurt her physically; that she'd gained at least *that* much control over herself.

Sanji looked on with fascination as Leslie stood her ground, and Ryan began to concede hers. The whip went limp in her grasp, then the arms unfolded, the eyes cooled slightly. Sanji knew she was safe now, from the beating anyway. But Ryan was still quite angry.

For the moment, Sanji's estimation of her Mistress grew. Leslie had achieved a revived sense of self since her out-of-body experience; she seemed stronger, better able to go on. The admiration was short-lived, however. When Sanji saw Ryan's spindly fingers run through her hair, she knew something had gone wrong. Not again, she thought, and proceeded to blame her Mistress for what would happen next. To Sanji, a beating, no matter how severe, was preferable to . . . "No," she breathed.

Ryan gave one last flashing glance at her wife, a tempermental flick of her whip which sounded against her pantleg, and walked briskly toward her den.

Leslie's shoulders deflated and she sighed angrily. "Damn," she whispered through clenched teeth. She might have known Ryan would turn to Anara at a time like this. But she couldn't stand idly by and allow Sanji to be mishandled. She had to try to stop it, even if it meant her rival would benefit from it.

She lifted Sanji to her feet, giving a closer look to the wound on her face. Mindful of her place, Sanji averted her eyes, and submitted to the inspection. No one hated Anara more than she did. The thought of her Master spending even a second in that detestable demi-goddess' clutches sickened her. But when Leslie handled her so tenderly, Sanji's heart softened. She replied forgivingly with a tiny squeeze to her Mistress' hand, realizing that she wasn't the only one who paid the price for this rescue. Leslie would sleep alone tonight, too.

4

Blaise gave a soft sigh of fulfillment. Her climax had been euphoric and she reveled in the afterglow, then shuddered as Anara removed her hands from where they had been, allowing one to travel up Blaise's spine; the other, more searchingly, up her belly to pause at her splendid wine-colored nipples.

Anara gathered the naked body of her lover into her arms, keeping her in a loving embrace as she gazed into Blaise's receptive red eyes. She took the hand that had recently been buried in Blaise's dark sex and smoothed it over the firm, wavy mass of charcoal hair which framed this enchanting oval face. Blaise looked vulnerable now; Anara preferred it that way. Even when they had been lovers on the physical plane some three thousand years ago, Anara had been the dominant half of the relationship, the teacher. Blaise had always been the willing student, able to please. And how pleasing she is, Anara thought lustily as she began to part her own robes to make way for the reciprocal, and equally competent, act of woman love.

Blaise found it was difficult to withdraw her gaze from Anara's spellbinding white eyes which looked even more dramatic when she was surrounded by the rich, royal purples of her bedchamber and plentiful robes. Her black tresses were lost in the shadows and creases of plush velvet. The light-swallowing effect was offset to an even higher degree when Anara revealed her *pure* white skin and amber-tipped breasts.

When this sight entered Blaise's peripheral vision, she felt the draw, the loud whisper of need calling her to lose herself in the mind-tampering ecstasy of Anara's body.

With her own satisfaction to shore her up, Blaise was able to hold her thirsting mouth just above the hardened tip of nirvana. Her tongue slid out to make the lightest of contact with it, then retracted.

Anara would have no part of the teasing effort. She grabbed Blaise by the hair and forced her head into her cushion of womanliness to the accompaniment of hoarse moans.

Blaise was buried in velvet skin and robes and loving it.

The knock went unnoticed, ignored. Then it went away. Anara continued her sexual tussle with Blaise, mindless of her surroundings and wholly unaware that she was being watched. Luckily for the viewer, Anara's ascent to rapture was unimpeded. The shrill exclamation of delight and release filled the plush room and the minds of all within hearing.

Anara didn't miss a beat when, with Blaise still burrowed into her sated flesh, she hurled the nearest heavy object at her handmaiden, Fila. "What are you doing in here? You jealous, voyeuristic tramp!"

Fila, pride of her Amazonian race, deftly dodged the tangible missile but not the verbal one. She was jealous, and hated having that fact show. It was not, as Anara tried to imply, that she was unwelcome in this mysterious boudoir. Quite the contrary: she had been well-received in this voluminous bed for far longer than its current visitor, *well*-received. Voyeur? Yes, she was. Another attribute of her race. Even still, the only pleasure she took from visually scanning the scene before her was the defenseless, exposed posture of Blaise's nude body: splayed out, belly down, head lodged between thighs which had yet to pry apart to free their captive. But tramp? Never.

She had taken a chance by entering the love nest unbidden, but felt the risk worth the final outcome. She grew more certain as she watched her queen settle into her masses of pillows, a sly grin beginning to conquer her beautiful salmon-tinted lips. Languor weighed down Anara's eyelids; the whole effect was very sexy to Fila.

It was meant to be. Anara purposely left herself exposed, and reached down to pat Blaise's head as one would an obedient pet.

Blaise controlled her angry response to such treatment—Anara's temper was legendary and only worth arousing at great cost. Moments after pleasing her (no mean feat) was not the time to allow personal humiliation to displace the overall feeling of contentment and love, however tarnished by bitchiness it might be. Blaise arranged her gaze over the plane of the snowy stomach into one of admiration, and waited.

"I suppose you have a reason for this ill-timed entry," Anara mocked as she inspected her slender fingers.

Fila stepped forward, certain now that her news would please her Mistress. At one time she had felt kindly toward her rival, Blaise, a product of their past association on the physical plane. But that had changed, and Fila was more than ready to place this fiery woman who, by all rights, should be an enemy of Anara, in disfavor with her.

"I do, my Queen. If I may direct your attention to the physical world for a moment . . . " Fila said with a hopeful tone, knowing all the while she had Anara's undivided attention.

"Yes, yes. What for?" Anara prodded impatiently. She was beginning to enjoy this situation inadvertently created by her servant.

"The One Who Seeks Knowledge and Justice, my Queen . . ." Fila hesitated, waiting for Anara's interest to sharpen further still.

Anara parted her legs easily, as though her lover were forgotten, and sat upright. That Fila would continue was taken for granted.

Out of the corner of her eye, Fila kept watch for Blaise's reaction as she revealed: "has removed the Veils that kept her earthly location obscured from us all." Fila made a courtly gesture designed to present the setting below.

Anara's response was as hasty as it was predictable: she thrust open her heavy drapes and scanned the planetary surface. It took scarcely no time for her to find what she was looking for. There, in the same town, the same *house* as Blaise's physical embodiment of Ryan, was the peacefully asleep incarnation of The One Who Seeks Knowledge and Justice—Leslie Anne Serle.

Again the most inevitable reaction: Anara turned on Blaise.

Fila enjoyed it all too thoroughly. As she made her proclamation, Blaise had been getting dressed. Blaise turned suddenly and briefly to Fila, registering her disbelief. Her fingers worked the buttons of her robe at breakneck speed while she made a quick glance earthward. She knew where to look, always had known. Her own physical body was in a state of trance in her den, and her beautiful, earthly wife was asleep in the master suite. It had been her hope that The One Who Seeks Knowledge and Justice, Queen Regent of the Throne of Council, would never see fit to disclose her earthly whereabouts. It would have been a lot safer under the circumstances.

Blaise was not surprised by the vicious blow to her face or the shouts and accusations of treason. She was hurt and frightened, and disappeared into a crackling blaze of fire, then extinguished even that facet of herself.

Before Anara could vent any more of her fury on her lover, Blaise was gone. She and Fila were stunned by the suddenness of the action. Neither of them knew Blaise to possess such an ability. The expediency of the act left Anara no one to take her rage out on but Fila, who caught it full force.

The simplest, most readily available method of punishment Anara had at her disposal was the seemingly inanimate copper serpent coiled about Fila's strong neck. The bronze-skinned giantess was brought humbly to her knees, choking and gasping, to wrestle with this snake that, without warning, had life breathed into it. The reptilian necklace had but one function: to tighten or expand as willed by Anara, and two purposes: to punish, and to serve as an ever present reminder to its wearer just *who* she belonged to.

The gruesome struggle ended with Fila collapsed unconscious at the foot of Anara's bed, the necklace once again metallic, without life.

Alone now, Anara could think and reflect. This new twist required some calculation on her part. But first, she needed to persuade Blaise to return to her bed.

"Blaise, my darling," Anara called in a voice that came as close to resembling begging as Anara would ever come. "I did not mean to harm you. You know my temper . . . it serves me well at times and ill at others. Do forgive my rash actions. Return to my sweet arms, and let me comfort you. I am calm now, and will not hurt you." She knew it was only a matter of time before her lover would relent. Blaise was always prepared to forgive, even gullible upon occasion.

Before long, Blaise materializd in Anara's open arms, ready to be soothed and healed, reinstated in her lover's esteem. While

Anara cooed to and stroked Blaise, she spoke nothing of forgiveness for the treachery of keeping silent about the identity of the Queen Regent. She wasn't *that* contrite.

Blaise paid the oversight no mind. Anara wasn't mad at her any longer, and that was all that mattered. Not once had she taken the trouble to make a justification for throwing Venadia over for Anara. She never stopped to analyze her actions; she had simply allowed herself to get caught up in the power of Anara's charm and devastating appeal. It was a thing of the moment, and Blaise didn't think beyond any of it, just felt it.

She knew why Venadia had disclosed her whereabouts on the physical side: to keep from being discovered by some being who was clever enough to solve the mystery at some point when Venadia might be off guard or unprepared. The Queen Regent had wisely taken the offensive, showing herself to be courageous, and someone to be reckoned with.

Anara's theories weren't so accurate. To Anara's self-important way of thinking, the Queen Regent had seen fit to unVeil herself because she stood no chance of winning back Blaise's love, and had dropped out of the running. In addition, the very fact that she, Anara, was now lovers with Blaise eliminated any reason for the Queen Regent to choose sides in the battle that was no longer going to be fought.

Her mind turned to the mundane. *So that's why I've never been able to frighten that little blonde wench away from Blaise's physical self,* she consoled herself. For close to two years she had been trying to put a stop to Leslie's determined efforts to stay by Ryan's side, come what may, with positively no success. It was no longer a mystery to her why her opponent hadn't responded in a fashion in keeping with typical female behavior. *She's not a typical female. And I thought I was losing my touch.* With that congratulatory thought, Anara turned her loving, contented gaze upon the delightful woman in her arms. Her last reasoning thought before stirring Blaise to more arduous lovemaking was that perhaps *now* the wench would leave.

Friday—and for some reason Ryan had undertaken to overhaul her classic Harley Davidson—which had worked flawlessly since Ryan had acquired it when she was fifteen years old. She and her mechanic, Bernie, had been hard at it since early in the morning, and they had both been drinking since they had begun. Beer, Leslie noted with relief as she stood in the doorway of the garage watching her mate cleaning a part with great care. Neither woman was likely to get drunk on beer, a fact Leslie considered when she concocted the bogus errand for Bernie that would leave her alone with Ryan for a short time.

Leslie was more than glad to see Ryan involved in something concrete that would occupy her mind as well as her time. There was something hopeful in this scene, something less self-destructive. Applying her infallible logic, Leslie thought ahead, as Ryan may not have, to the fact that if the chopper were in pieces about the garage floor for what could amount to days, then it wouldn't be available to get her to the bars all weekend. And as proud as Ryan was, she would *not* drive the Rolls Royce to the sleazy dives she had been frequenting. Nor would she ask to use Leslie's sporty Mercedes, and Ryan hated driving trucks, so Bernie's vehicle wasn't a possibility. She would still go, but not under her own power.

Ryan didn't seek out Leslie's company any more. Unless she wanted sex. Meals together were infrequent, taken quickly, endured in palpable silence. If Leslie wanted to be with Ryan she had to find ways to place herself in Ryan's path, and then only when she could summon the courage. Ryan's path was harm's way more often than not.

The frame of the motorcycle was mounted on a sturdy structure that allowed for plenty of maneuvering room. There was but one place for Leslie to go to make sure Ryan would even look at her.

"Good morning," she greeted carefully.

Before Ryan could acknowledge or ignore her, Leslie found her way onto the seat of the motorcycle. She tested the perch for steadiness and found it quite suitable, then relaxed. Ambushes rarely failed with Ryan. She knew how to get her lover's attention as well as Sanji did. Her shapely legs glided into the Irishwoman's line of vision.

Ryan was in a catcher's crouch inspecting the part in her hand, but she put it on the floor in an absentminded way when she spied khaki green, lizard pumps coyly and deliberately inserted before her eyes. Unable to resist the call of her senses, she followed the line of the most beautiful legs she'd ever seen (dressed with pastel brown stocking so sheer they could have been airbrushed on) to the hem of the jacquard silk dress and beyond. The cocoa fabric shimmered in the light as Leslie moved seductively, calling attention to the wide sash tied about her hips in a designed-to-be-challenging manner. The poof sleeves and tight, prim collar kept up the taunt. The whole "I dare you" look made Ryan smile. Maybe she wouldn't wipe the grease off her hands after all.

"Well, good morning," Ryan replied, her voice slightly lower than her regular speaking voice.

Leslie smiled in return, purposely ignoring Ryan's notice of her. "What prompted you to perform major surgery on your bike?" she asked, half-seriously. She knew her grey eyes had a wry glint to them, and did nothing to dampen it. Ryan had no idea just how close to her she was, what easy prey.

Ryan lit a cigarette, and picked up a wrench to toy with while she earnestly contemplated her reason for dismantling her machine.

Leslie knew that, more than any plausible one, the real reason was because Ryan needed Bernie's company — someone like herself who knew what it was to be a masculine woman. Now, more than ever. With her old friend Rags dead, and not on speaking terms with her cousin, the gap yawned empty and tragically before her. It was a need Ryan couldn't verbalize. Instead she put forth: "Seems I read in a manual once that after eighteen years Harley Davidsons *fell* apart, so I thought, why wait?"

They both chuckled, each glad to hear the other laugh. Ryan's gaze slid longingly back to the lizard pumps with their stunning scalloped uppers.

Leslie felt a wicked smile tremble on her lips. This was why she had come to the garage. For as long as she'd known Ryan, she'd known Ryan had a shoe fetish. Curiously, unlike her other passions, something kept Ryan at a distance from this refined desire. The distance had been narrowing, to be certain, but still a veil of inhibition separated Ryan from the complete fulfillment of her need.

In recent months Leslie had been encouraged to acquire vast numbers of pairs of shoes. An easy task for her because she loved shoes, and her tastes corresponded precisely with her lover's.

The closet where these hallowed objects resided was frequented increasingly more often by the undenied ruler of McKinley. It was not uncommon to find her sitting in a chair, smok-

49

ing a cigarette, trying to appear casual, and watching. Watching as Corelle cleaned, buffed, arranged (admired), and cared for each of Leslie's shoes. Leslie never minded. She was always the beneficiary of Ryan's artificially stimulated state of need.

Leslie cleared her throat to draw attention away from her feet. In the brief moment when Ryan looked up at her, she extended her foot between Ryan's spread knees and rubbed the toe of her pump firmly up and down Ryan's crotch.

The wrench clanged to the floor, the cigarette fell behind it and rolled away, and the force of Ryan's staggering passion drove her knees hard into the concrete. Her breath wheezed out of her as though she had been hit in the stomach.

Leslie calculatedly crossed over the line, willfully folding back Ryan's last resistance. She answered the almost painful look of pleading on her mate's face with a simple and determined command. *"Fuck* it, Ryan."

"Ohh, goaahd," Ryan gasped. She forgot entirely about the grease on her fingers as she entwined them around the heel and arch of the glorious shoe. With no more hesitation, she thrust the object into her sex, pinning the toe of the shoe and Leslie's instep between her vicelike thighs while she took her longing for a wild and furious ride. A ride she needed to take and couldn't, until Leslie had given her the permission she'd been unable to give herself.

Leslie steadied herself for the jarring, tearing fit of Ryan's rut. It took every bit of her strength, but she managed to bear up as Ryan looked skyward, beseeching the heavens for this bliss to go on to its most thrilling conclusion. It did. To the strains of the animal sounds of carnal joy Ryan was given to when rocked by extreme pleasure and release.

By now, Ryan cared nothing for harsh realities: the grease on her hands as they made loving trails up stockinged legs; that Bernie was due back soon. She had one thing in mind and one thing only: Leslie's blonde sex. She took the dare Leslie's elegantly sophisticated dress issued, picked up the gauntlet this saucy, aloof ensemble threw down.

Within seconds her agile hands sought their way up the thighs and under the fabric. Leslie put up no fight as the searching fingers deftly urged her hips off the motorcycle seat to lay open the path for the panties to be removed by this virtuoso. There was no need for words, the lingerie was simply peeled down the legs and pocketed in Ryan's jacket.

Ryan wanted Leslie, and the dress, to know who was boss here. Yes, she had been outwitted by her wife, and was grateful. Never again would she feel the pressure-cooker emotions that restraining her fetish had produced. The relief of that freedom was beyond description for her.

She'd been bushwhacked by women before, and would be again, but she always came out on top. And this time was no different. Again, her hands made the soft journey up Leslie's thighs, but this time she took the hem of the skirt with her— above Leslie's waist.

Now her wife was exposed, helpless, and very wet. Her passionate fragrance was well in evidence, as was her growing need.

"Invite me," came Ryan's rough demand.

Leslie hastened to comply, spreading the lips of her sex wide, her subtly painted fingertips flanking her hardened focus of pleasure and glistening entrance to all that is woman.

Leslie's moans were disproportionately loud for the light touch of Ryan's tongue. Ryan stiffened her organ and pushed it inside, bringing the creamy arousal out where she could spread it about Leslie's pinkness. Before long neither of them were aware of their surroundings as Leslie's fingers were now grinding into the back of Ryan's head, her thighs balanced on her lover's shoulders, Ryan's mouth now devouring her goodness. Her tongue and lips took a thorough massaging when Leslie's body cried out its blessed satisfaction. Ryan sat back on her heels, lit two cigarettes and passed one to her happy wife.

A fully suspended moment elapsed after they heard Bernie's gruff cough before Ryan made a move to preserve her wife's modesty by pulling the skirt over her private area. Bernie had been leaning against the entrance to the garage and, after Leslie took her legs off Ryan's shoulders, she busied herself looking for a tool she didn't need.

No one uttered a word, but more than one pleased smile passed between them before Leslie left the two mechanics to their work and their beer and their friendly conversation.

5

October was Leslie's favorite time of the year, especially when the weather was as spectacular as it had been the past few days: warm, clear and fragrant. The extensive grounds of McKinley had been putting on a final show of the year: golden leaves, late-blooming roses, any and every plant that had anything left in it saw fit to bloom for Leslie. She had whiled away her morning celebrating life, acknowledging each and every flower, thanking the Goddess of Beauty for looking kindly upon this estate she shared with her lover.

Now, as the afternoon began to wane she was paying tribute to the less showy aspects of their grounds. She was sketching the giant weeping willow with its tears of gold, and the rushes, dandelions and asters playing about in the tree's shadow.

That her thirty-fifth birthday was a week off was something she tried to ignore. Thinking about it only made it more difficult to be emotionally separated from the woman she loved more than life.

She satisfied herself, instead, with the occasional visit to or from a friend, and the constant companionship of one or both of her handmaidens, Corelle and Sanji. They were with her now: Corelle knitting, Sanji writing a letter to her family in Jamaica.

It was all the more jarring then, when into this quietude

entered the noise of car wheels grinding to a halt on the gravel cart path several yards from where the three women sat engaged in their solitary occupations. In unison their heads lifted and turned toward the fire-red Aston Martin Volante convertible, duplicating each other's thoughts: Outstanding car. *What* is Brigid doing here?

Leslie could almost feel her maids' hackles rise in tandem with her own. "If I'd meant for cars to use that path, I'd have had it made wider," Leslie breathed maliciously. The sports car had only just kept from ripping the turf bordering the path. Leslie had to admit that it had been a good bit of driving, which kept her from realizing that there was something amiss here. Still, she wondered, why had Brigid come? Ryan was home. Surely she had seen that on her way to this distant part of McKinley. And that is a very determined walk for someone who is normally easy-going. It wasn't until the redhead sat down too close to her that Leslie realized what was wrong. Dead wrong.

"You've been drinking," Leslie said uncordially. She felt her companions shift uneasily behind her. They knew the story well of how Ryan's cousin had lost her leg in a drunken car accident. How she had sworn off drinking for ten years until her lover and paramour had both left her. But even that one episode had been the exception. Brigid hadn't been known to taste another drop since that time.

Brigid let the comment pass. "Hello, Leslie." She waited for a reply, and when it wasn't forthcoming she picked up the sketch Leslie had been working on. Despite her rapid heartbeat and sweaty palms, her highly trained artistic eye served her well. There was room for improvement in the sketch, but Leslie was learning more all the time. All in all, it was a very good rendering, which didn't surprise Brigid in the least. Everything Leslie did, she did well.

Leslie recovered her sense of reason quickly. If she'd learned nothing else from living with Ryan, it was that it didn't pay to be critical of someone's drinking. She softened her tone considerably. "Well, what do you think?" she asked genuinely.

Brigid nodded her head favorably, looking then at the object of her visit. "It's quite good. You've come a long way in the short time since you picked up this interest."

Trying to steer the conversation away from what was so obviously portrayed in Brigid's grey eyes, Leslie commented, "The

54

advice and tips you've given to me have been invaluable. Have any more?" she asked hopefully.

Brigid placed her hand over Leslie's. "Come to study with me," she suggested boldly. She let her eyes scan Leslie's soft, ivory silk blouse and navy skirt and up again to meet the almost curious expression on her friend's face.

It suddenly became very important for Leslie to determine not only how much her unwelcome suitor had been drinking, but of what? Never mind why; she suspected she knew the answer to that. It smelled like whiskey which, if Brigid were anything like Ryan, she might be in for a tough time. If she thought about it, the answer to her first question was obvious. Like Ryan, Brigid didn't do anything half-way. Chances were very good that she'd had more than she could safely handle.

Leslie pulled her hand away gently, answering shyly, "I couldn't."

Brigid raised her voice causing Sanji and Corelle to fidget restlessly. "You *could*, you *won't*," she rejoined bitterly.

Leslie's plan was not working. Of all possible times to be stubborn with a drunken Irishwoman, this was the worst. But she heard herself saying, almost against her will, "Perhaps I can have someone drive you home, Brig." Leslie was insulted by the redhead's tone.

Brigid was just a millimeter from losing her temper as well, which was not what she wanted. "I'll go home . . . " she ventured. Leslie cooled slightly, thinking she'd made the right move after all. "If you'll drive me there." She reached for the dainty hand again, but it was pulled abruptly from her grasp.

"This is absurd. I'll go summon a car for you myself." Leslie made a move to stand up, but was grabbed meanly above the elbow, and brought back down to her seated position.

"You're not going anywhere," Brigid stated threateningly.

Leslie's mouth opened breathlessly, her eyes grew large with surprise and wonder. Corelle took in her breath also, but covered the thin yelp with her hand. Sanji's mind worked quickly, exploring the possibilities. She didn't know Brigid well, all she'd seen of her had been her basically sound, stable artist personality. She had heard of the fights Ryan and her cousin had shared at the bars in days gone by, so she knew Brigid was capable of violence—but not against someone she loved and cherished. Bloodlines told, and this woman had been drinking. She sized up her chances of helping her Mistress if things went sour,

55

which they looked like they might. Corelle was no help—the dear thing was a true lamb. While strong, Sanji was no match for the virile redhead. Brigid's metal crutches were handy . . . if she dare strike her Master's cousin. There was only the one choice, and she was prepared to take it if her Mistress couldn't outsmart her guest.

"Let go of me," Leslie ordered, but the spirit wasn't upon her as it had been the last time she'd encountered this situation. Her words were impotent. There was a red halo around Brigid's eyes now, and Leslie knew for certain that the time for courtship was over, sensibility flown by.

Brigid had rounded the corner of her mission, and there was no looking back. She was going to have Leslie. Period.

With a slight shake of her head she replied coolly, "No."

It all happened so fast that Sanji couldn't get to her feet before it was too late. Brigid was remarkably agile for a drunken woman with one leg. In one swift, fluid movement she was on top of Leslie tearing away her blouse and mashing her lips with kisses she'd stored up for months of endless nights.

Sanji was gone. Corelle pounded foolishly on Brigid's broad back trying to get her to stop, pleading in Irish, crying tears of panic and desperation.

At first, Leslie had been stunned out of action. Brigid's shocking weight forced the breath out of her, and, strangely, there had been something astonishingly familiar about Brigid's presence—so very much like Ryan's—that she didn't realize it wasn't Ryan.

When she became aware of what was going on, she struggled to free herself with all her might. She managed to scream once, twice, when Brigid's mouth moved to her naked breast. But a free and very large hand smothered her next and subsequent screams.

A mean mouth descended upon her soft breast, bruising it, biting the nipple. Leslie's mind cried out that this wasn't really happening to her, it couldn't be. But when a viscious and resolute hand—too large, and roughened by years of ceramic work—forced open her legs and jabbed into her sex, her mind left off thinking and reverted to animalism. There was only pain, and the fight.

Brigid was insane. Her mind was playing convenient tricks on her to keep her from an awareness of what she was really doing. To her deranged mind, she was consumating her love for this woman. Leslie's struggle was translated to her as writhing passion. Her victim's muffled screams reached her ears as moans of pleasure and lust. The harder Leslie struggled and screamed, the more Brigid sought to satisfy this hallucination of love's completion.

Ryan and Bernie had settled into a comfortable rhythm, working as a team to overhaul Ryan's motorcycle. They enjoyed one another's company. Bernie was especially glad to be admitted into Ryan's inner circle of friends — Ryan confided in her more and more, which made her feel special. Watching the private workings of Ryan's household fascinated Bernie, and she didn't mind the excellent pay (or the fringe benefits). She liked Ryan, respected her, and relished every chance she was given to be around her. More than once she'd caught herself just staring at Ryan's hands, amazed by their dexterity in making mechanical repairs and adjustments.

She was staring just then when Ryan looked up suddenly, a quizzical, alert expression animating her face.

"Did you hear something?" Ryan asked Bernie with vague immediacy.

Bernie didn't know what she could have heard that was unusual. The radio and the rattle of their work made all the noises she'd been listening to. "No, nothing out of the ordinary."

"There, there it is again." Ryan listened for the severe interruption to her senses to happen again as she stood to turn off the radio. It was quiet now, but only outside Ryan's brain. In her mind she was hearing cries of pain. Without realizing it, she was both feeling Leslie's pain and experiencing her cousin's violent insanity.

For no apparent reason, she began to sweat, and turned two full shades whiter than her already startlingly pale complexion. Bernie rose to her feet, concerned. "Ryan?" she asked fearfully. "Are you all right?"

Before she could move closer, Sanji arrived in a frenzy at the door to the garage. Ryan came to herself at the sight of her.

"Master, come quickly," she pleaded frantically. "My Lady is being taken against her will!"

Ryan sprang into action immediately, grabbing Sanji by the shoulders. "Where?" she demanded.

"By the weeping willow tree."

Almost before the words were spoken, Ryan had taken off at a full run toward the southern end of McKinley, followed by Sanji and Bernie.

Fueled by adrenalin, Ryan wasn't aware of the hedges she hurdled or of the speed with which she traversed the distance. Nor was she surprised to find the criminal was her own cousin. She wasn't thinking, just acting to save her wife from harm.

When she arrived on the scene she shoved Corelle out of the way and yanked Brigid off Leslie, then fell upon Brigid, pounding her fists into her face. Brigid fought back blindly and injuriously.

Sanji made it seconds after Ryan; her goal was Leslie who, once freed from the attack upon her person, curled into a fetal ball, sobbing painfully. Sanji and Corelle sheltered her from danger, and began to comfort her with little or no success.

Bernie charged into the battle and assumed command. She'd ended more than one fight where Ryan and Brigid had been participants, although she never thought she'd see the day when they would be fighting each other. Using sheer brute force, she pulled the opponents apart, jerking Ryan to her feet and out of reach of Brigid, at the same time kicking the metal crutches, which she'd seen do real damage before, out of the redhead's reach.

"God damn it, Ryan, stop it!" Bernie boomed. "Leslie needs you." Bernie butted her palms against Ryan's shoulders shoving her away, jarring some sense into her.   •

Her words went straight home. Ryan blinked away her fury and rage, and let her eyes rest on her frightened, hurt wife. Instantly she was filled with compassion and the desire to comfort her. Corelle and Sanji moved away to let Ryan hold Leslie, but when she touched her wife, Leslie screamed and jumped away crying, "No more, please, no. No more!"

Ryan took a deep breath to calm herself, then began to speak soothingly to her heart of hearts. "Angel, it's me, Ryan. I won't hurt you. Let me hold you, please. Let me caress you in my arms, sweet darling. I love you."

Finally Leslie registered the voice, recognized it, responded to it. She let Ryan approach her, then she curled up in the lap that awaited her and the succor that was unlike any other available—true relief from pain. Ryan gathered the trembling body and shaken spirit into the folds of her healing touch, rocking the victim, whispering softly to her.

Brigid was used to being brought out of violent episodes by Bernie; she accepted the assistance with relief. She let Bernie help her to her feet and into her crutches, but nothing could rescue her from the dawning realization of what she had just done. Bernie sized up her beaten face, easily able to guess what Ryan's would look like the next day. Brigid pulled a handkerchief from her pocket to wipe the blood from the cut above her eye which was beginning to smart now that she didn't have insanity to block the pain.

Hoping to avoid a scene, Bernie tried to nudge Brigid toward her car so she could drive the stunned woman home. Stubbornly, Brigid turned to face Ryan and Leslie. She wanted to say she was sorry, but the look of hatred on Ryan's face froze the words in her mouth.

Ryan pulled Leslie tight to her body with one hand, and pointed a warning finger at Brigid with the other. "Come near her again and you're a dead woman," Ryan told her in a bone-chilling tone that said to all within hearing that she was not only capable of killing her cousin, but that she was seriously considering it.

The threat from Ryan didn't worry Brigid as much as the lack of response from Leslie. Just how hurt she was was evidenced by the fact that she didn't object to Ryan's ominous words.

Shocked, Brigid allowed herself to be guided to her car and placed meekly into the passenger seat. Bernie got in the car and drove carefully away, clenching her teeth against her own anger. She alone had seen the blood on Brigid's hand, and the teeth marks on the palm of her other. Like all who came into the scope of service to Ryan O'Donnell, she felt duty-bound to do the best thing even in the worst times. Making certain that Brigid was taken home safely and not left alone was perhaps the hardest thing Bernie had ever done, but she could see the writing on the wall. Ryan might not thank her for saving Brigid's life now, but she might someday.

Sanji, meanwhile, had had the presence of mind to find a flatbed gardening cart. She drove the electric vehicle up to the grassy area where Ryan sat with Leslie, then got off to help Corelle who was mute and traumatized. Stuporous, Corelle let herself be moved onto the back of the cart while Ryan sat in the front with Leslie cradled in her arms. Sanji drove them away from the once beloved place—a spot on McKinley's grounds where none of the four of them would return to, where everything eventually would wither and die, where nothing would grow again.

Hatred prompted Sanji to break the silence of their journey back to the main part of the mansion. "Master, did Anara do this?" she asked with a grim voice. She could almost *feel* Leslie's spine tighten. The question popped Corelle's bubble of hypnosis; she turned about to hear Ryan's response.

Ryan saw the way of it then. It hadn't occurred to her, it never did until it was too late, that this horrifying event was the left-over product of one of Anara's old, demented tricks. A loose end that Anara had forgotten to tie up when she and Ryan's spirit self, Blaise, had fallen in love. Suddenly, all the old hatred she had felt for her nemesis flooded back into her. Her recall for destesting that white-eyed oppressor became vivid and clear. How foolish she had been to believe that Anara was ever really capable of true love. Even more to forget that she had true love, right there in her grasp, all the while. Love that wouldn't die, wasn't capricious, was unswerving, and all hers.

Ryan sighed, kissed Leslie's head and looked to the horizon. She knew what she had to do now. She began her resolution to rebuild that love before she lost it entirely by replying, "Yes, it was."

"Corelle, listen to me." Ryan had taken over all aspects of her wife's healing process with authority. Among the many necessary components that went into making up the journey back to emotional, physical and spiritual health was regaining a sense of purpose and routine. Corelle's purpose in life was to serve, and Ryan needed her to fulfill it, knowing that giving the girl specific duties to carry out would hasten her back to life and health as well. "Draw a bath of clear, hot water for your Mistress, undress her (burn the clothes), then help her into her bath. I shall be there shortly."

Still mildly dazed, Corelle replied unquestioningly, "Yes, Master," and scurried off to her tasks.

Ryan looked in on Leslie, who was lying on the chaise in her boudoir, watched carefully by Sanji. Reassured, Ryan stripped off her clothing and took herself to her shower where she could wash the mechanical grime as well as any trace of her angry attack upon her cousin from her body.

Corelle looked up from the sunken marble bath she had just eased Leslie into to see Ryan standing before her dressed in a long, black and gold robe, hair wet and combed back tight against her scalp. Ryan drew Corelle to her feet, motioned Sanji to come to her, then spoke softly to her faithful charges. "Clean yourselves, change your clothes and take a nourishing meal. If we require anything, I'll call." With gentle kisses she sent them away, closing the door behind them.

After lighting a scented candle, closing the drapes, putting on some recorded harp music, Ryan let her robe fall to the floor and she joined her wife in the hot bath.

Ryan took advantage of her presence being unrecognized to utter a healing incantation, spoken in the Old Tongue. She took Leslie's favorite shampoo from the ledge next to the candle and began to wash her wife's silky blonde hair. Ryan was nearly finished with the entire cleansing of hair and body before the vacant and distant look began to fade from Leslie's face.

Gradually, the patient's head turned toward the healer, the mind at last making out who was there with her. It was dark in the room except for the small flame throwing dancing light on the well-carved face she loved so dearly. To convince herself there was a real person next to her, Leslie brought her hand from the water and ran it through the partially dry strands of Ryan's jet-black hair. She checked to make certain the head was attached to a body because Ryan had never joined her in the expansive bath before. Her eyes rose, seeking the final proof: the magnificently powerful, jade eyes of her lover.

Those eyes were real and wide open to her, caressing her, loving her, adoring her, offering the balm of devotion, begging forgiveness, letting her back in where she'd been shut out from for so very long. The two fit a lifetime into the drawn out span of time wherein they silently respoke their marriage vows, lost in one another's eyes. This they followed with warm, welcoming kisses, discovering interplaying of fingers, the sighs of calm joy that spoke of love eternal. Love reborn, Love.

No longer separate, again as one, they rose from the tepid water to towel off. Ryan lifted her wife into her arms and carried her to the master suite where she would begin the next phase of the healing. She made her way through the vast, darkened room easily, to the large teak bed she shared with the beloved woman in her arms.

After relaxing under the covers for a time, Ryan approached what she knew would be the hardest part for Leslie, but once she was past the most frightening hurdle the patient would begin to heal on all levels. Ryan knew as well as anyone that when a trauma occurred in the course of doing something that ordinarily came naturally, the best thing was to resume that activity again as soon as possible. The first time she'd dumped her motorcycle, she'd forced herself to pick it up again and drive it on, even though she was in pain and badly shaken. Leslie, a victim of a crime of sexual violence, could not be allowed to avoid sex. She had to go on, learning the difference between sexual love and sexual rape.

At first, Leslie wasn't quite aware she was being kissed; Ryan's lips were so light, feathery, affectionate. She closed her eyes as the caresses passed over them. Her whole face was annointed, then her neck, shoulders, arms. Each finger was taken and worshipped by the adoring mouth. Her sides, abdomen, thighs became the beneficiaries of the roaming, albeit thorough coating of sweet kisses. A gentle stirring milled through her heart then headed downward. It was all so innocent that Leslie made no move to prevent the adornment of her legs, feet, toes, arches.

Floating dreamily she let Ryan turn her over onto her stomach. The tiny sparks started small fires as the lips smoothed over her rounded backside, kindled large fires up the spine; deepened breathing ensued when the tongue made its first appearance, darting quickly in her ear.

Once again on her back, Leslie became acutely aware that of all the wonderful places that had been paid homage to, her breasts and sex were not among them. Now on the border between the healing attentions of her mate and the lust-quickening teasing of her lover, Leslie still hesitated, needing encouragement.

Sensing this, Ryan let her lips brush the tender underside of Leslie's conical-shaped breast, "accidently" letting the tip of her nose skim the taut surface of her alert nipple. To this temptation she added a faint, but very obviously restrained moan. The invitation met with acceptance as Leslie moved into the second brush, which just *happened* to find Ryan's hot, breathy mouth directly in the path of an increasingly needier nipple. The goading mouth fanned the flame in both breasts then descended to the golden tuft between Leslie's legs. Here Leslie was not so successful at getting what she wanted without asking for it. Here the tongue and lips maintained a holding pattern, circling in even paths over the thighs and belly, but never, never even breezing the excited hairs of her sex. Ryan deftly dodged any attempt Leslie made to place herself in the trek of her patient provocation.

When fear was conquered by desire the result swept them both away. Leslie grabbed Ryan's head between her hands and forcefully guided her lover's gifted mouth into her willing sex. Between Leslie's hisses of delight and Ryan's moans of renewed passion, neither of them cared how they got there, just as long as they could meet as quickly as possible in their private chapel of pleasure. Reunited, they met with the angels in celebration of marital bliss.

A fortnight would pass before the couple re-emerged from the connubial suite, refreshed, rejoined, their love rebuilt on a stronger foundation than before, ready to withstand all that would come their way.

"Lie down, or I'll deck ya, MacSweeney," Bernie ordered impatiently. Brigid had recovered from her shock, and was now as nervous as a cat, which was making Bernie nervous. Now that she'd gotten the offender home she didn't know what to do with her. Sitting around watching her pace wasn't what she had in mind.

Brigid halted her irritated stride abruptly. She measured Bernie's stern gaze—the fierce, narrowed eyes that meant business (and Bernie had punched out her fair share of aggressive dykes). Thwarted, Brigid obeyed, propping her crutches against the wall and burying her sore face in a pillow. With her body motionless she was all the more aware of the whirlpool of emotion that was trying to suck her into the vacuum of non-existence. She was horrified by her own actions, afraid of herself and what she might do or become. She knew she'd lost Ryan and Leslie as friends, possibly for all time. How could either of them ever forgive her? She was beginning to ask herself over and over, why she had done it. No answer would materialize. In her disorganized mental state, she didn't really expect a reason to form, possibly because she was too frightened to look at her darker self, to see that she may have *wanted* to force herself on Leslie. Or that she might still be so insecure that her irrational need to prove herself Ryan's equal would never be satisfied, even if Leslie had consented to see her privately. She touched on those fears and others, felt a nagging sense of self-pity, but mostly she was trying to run from herself and any truth she might encounter if she looked at any one thing too closely. Bernie's voice was a welcome respite from her self-involvement.

"Do you have any drugs?" Bernie asked. Her question was two-fold: Brigid needed something for pain, but didn't need to be alone where the easy way might be too tempting to ignore.

Brigid sighed. She knew what Bernie was driving at, and she doubted she could commit suicide, but she was beginning to see she didn't know herself quite as well as she had thought. "In the linen closet, just pain killers," she provided, subdued.

"Ice bag?"

"Under the kitchen sink."

Bernie brought a filled ice pack and a glass of water to Brigid. It cost Bernie to be kind to this woman she now despised. Her actions were rough and stingy as she handed her the pills; she was loathe to see them administered, preferring Brigid feel the pain of the beating Bernie wished she could have finished herself. But that wasn't how to take care of someone who was important to Ryan O'Donnell. Even still, the sincere look of gratitude on Brigid's face made her think that perhaps she was overreacting; there were a lot more positive sides of Brigid to consider.

All one had to do was look around the bright, airy loft Brigid called her home to see that this was a sensitive, caring woman. Plants abounded, cats were everywhere, or so it seemed when the three of them crowded around Brigid; fine art was a byword in this simple household. Brigid had earned national acclaim for her ceramics and watercolor paintings—even her oils had won notices. This was not the haunt of a common felon.

Bernie shook off her reverie, which was confusing her and doing nothing to find someone to look after this broken artist. She walked around the bed, took the telephone from the nightstand and walked into the kitchen nook with it to dial McKinley.

When the hearty Irish voice answered the call, Bernie began

to relax. Bonnie, the housekeeper, would know what to do; she'd known Ryan since birth and Brigid since early childhood.

"Bonnie, this is Bernie. I'm with Brigid, but I can't stay here all night. She shouldn't be alone." She didn't know if Bonnie had heard the tale yet. She suspected that Bonnie had, however, and would take things in hand; head housekeepers had a way of doing so.

"Oh, aye, she shouldn't, lass. If you can stay with her just a wee bit longer, I can have someone come to take care of her. Will ye do that for me?"

Bernie smiled. "Yes, dear. We'll be fine." She ended the conversation, placed the phone back where it belonged, and sighed, more from relief than weariness. Brigid had fallen asleep.

Bernie never would have suspected that the elegant woman opening the front door of Brigid's carriage house was Brigid's mother since there was no resemblance. Bernie had been sitting at the top of the stairs where she could keep an eye on Brigid and watch for her relief to arrive. She stood when the woman came into the shop area downstairs, below her.

"Evenin', ma'am," Bernie said as politely as she knew how.

Once she stood next to Bernie, the woman extended her hand graciously. "You're Bernie Valasquez?" To Bernie's nod she went on, "How do you do? I'm Aisling MacSweeney, Brigid's mother."

Bernie took the gloved hand in hers. "Pleased to meet you, Mrs. MacSweeney." A moment of uncomfortable silence hung between them while Aisling looked at her daughter on the bed. "What is wrong? Bonnie only said that my Brigid needed me, but wouldn't say why."

Bernie took in this beautiful woman, her copper-colored hair, delicate features, shocking sky blue eyes, and shook off her disbelief to answer, "It's not my place to say, ma'am." Bernie reached into her pocket, withdrew two brown vials, and handed them to the new arrival. "Here are all the pills I could find. I dumped her liquor. Here are her car keys. And I couldn't find a gun," Bernie stated flatly as though it were a common topic of discussion. For her it was. Babysitting unstable dykes was old hat to Bernie.

Aisling took the items reluctantly. "She doesn't shoot," she found herself saying dumbly. "I don't understand, Miss Valasquez. *What* is going on?"

"I think you ought to ask your daughter," Bernie dodged. She had had all she wanted of this situation, and then some. "I've got to run along, ma'am, if you'll excuse me?"

"Yes, yes. I'm sorry. Thank you, very much. I'm grateful for all your help. Is there anything I can do for you?" Aisling asked hopefully.

"Just don't leave her alone for a *minute*," Bernie instructed paternally. "I'll be going now."

Aisling put the pills and keys in her purse, wondering how Bernie was going to get home, then reasoning that McKinley was within walking distance for someone who had something on her mind to walk off. She looked at her daughter, and her heart sank.

"Oh, Bridie, what's ailin' you?" she whispered sorrowfully, using the nickname she hadn't spoken since Brigid was seven. She sat on the bed and reached for the aging orange tabby that had curled into the crook of Brigid's knee. The cat's complaint awakened Brigid.

When she turned toward her mother, Aisling sucked in her breath at the sight of Brigid's swelling face and darkening eyes. Dusk was eating the light; Brigid squinted to focus, then said oddly, "Mother?"

"Bridie, what's happened, darlin'?" Aisling pulled the Lilac point Siamese off Brigid's back so she could turn over. Brigid moved around to face her mother. Suddenly, upon hearing the childhood endearment, she wanted to confide in her mother, to be close to her, know the non-judgmental, perservering love of a mother. She needed the protective mantle only a mother could wrap around her weary shoulders and heart. She was safe now.

She yielded to the careful inspection of her mother's gentle fingers as they surveyed the strong, aching features of her proud face. "Who did this to you?" Aisling asked with a defensive tone. Her daughter had been hurt and she wanted some recourse. It hadn't occurred to her that Brigid was at fault.

"Ryan," Brigid answered, holding back her tears, uncertain if she could go on with the explanation.

"No." Aisling took her hand away, shaking her head. Ryan and Brigid had never fought, even as children. But Bonnie had been evasive, her voice had been shaky when she'd called. "Why, Bridie?" she asked suspiciously.

Brigid vaguely remembered Bernie washing the blood off her hand as she stroked it heavily against the calico cat next to her. She knew she couldn't look at her mother and still tell the truth.

And she couldn't lie to her no matter how much she wished she could.

"Because I . . . " Brigid closed her eyes, clenched her teeth and took a deep breath to conquer her tears, "forced my intentions on Leslie." She tried to listen to her calico purring instead of the dead stillness her mother had sucked into her mouth in surprise, then let out in something akin to disgust.

Aisling would never stop loving her daughter. She would stand by her now and all times she was called upon or needed, but she would not let Brigid get away with glossing over the facts. "You mean you raped her," Aisling correctly firmly.

Brigid had assumed her mother didn't know what rape was, or that a woman could do it to another woman. In that Brigid hadn't thought of her mother as a thinking, reasoning being with some experience beyond that of raising a family, she was no different than other daughters. But yes, she had *raped* Leslie, and nothing she could say or do would change that fact. It was something Brigid would have to live with for the rest of her life. She looked at her mother, accepting her fate. "I raped her."

After a brief look of compassion, Aisling stood and began busying herself about Brigid's loft. "You're coming to the south of France with me," she said suddenly, changing the topic skillfully.

"What?" Brigid asked, thoroughly nonplussed.

"There's no point in dwelling on any of this, Brigid. You need rest, fresh air, sunshine and a radical change of scenery."

"Mother . . . " Brigid objected obstinately.

Aisling whirled around and pointed a finger at her daughter. "Now listen here, young lady, you're headed straight for a nervous breakdown and a minimum of two years in the hospital, and I won't have it. You're coming home with me tonight; we'll pack tomorrow and leave the following day." Aisling knew that a vortex of activity and a chance to get things in perspective were the best medicines for her daughter's frayed nerves.

"But father . . . " Brigid reminded her mother of that which no one needed reminding: Brigid was still an outcast in the MacSweeney home.

"Your *father* . . . " Aisling emphasized bitterly, "is out of town."

"The cats . . . " Brigid added half-heartedly. She was beginning to warm to the idea.

Aisling motioned in the direction of the main estate Brigid's carriage house was attached to. "Will be taken care of, and will miss you less than if you were in a hospital."

Aisling rustled her charge out of bed and out of the lonely home, taking along only what was absolutely necessary, insisting that anything else could be found in France when they got there.

6

"That's the hardest thing I've ever done in my life." Delores Rhinehart took another sip from her double bourbon and slouched into her chair in front of the picture window which provided a spectacular view of Denver's glittering landscape. She had just been handed the biggest defeat of her life. And to compound the soul-emptying feeling she'd had to publicly acknowledge that defeat in front of all her supporters, the press, but worst of all, in front of her wife Dana Schaeffer.

If Dana were a compassionate woman, she would have been trying to offer her mate consolation, trying to encourage her to look to the future and other public offices, not sitting in her own chair scowling, sulking, staring at Denver's skyline and getting very drunk. She wouldn't be absorbed in her own consuming hatred for Leslie Serle and Ryan O'Donnell, nor would she be angry at Delores for losing the election for the seat in the State House of Representatives.

But Dana was *not* a compassionate woman. Del had learned to live with that in their many years together. Their relationship was a trade-off: Dana was a world class beauty, sinfully sexy, considered a prime catch, and Del was proud of being the one to have her. Del didn't try to make any sense out of her love for Dana; it was an addiction, and an expensive one at that. She would try for office again—she had to. Dana was as ambitious as she was beautiful, and part of what kept her around was Del's potential for becoming a highly respected citizen, holding one prestigious office after another as the years wore on. This was not an auspicious beginning, but she'd been up against a formidable opponent.

In all the years Del had known Leslie, she'd never thought her capable of revenge. She wanted to blame the change in Leslie on Ryan, but couldn't. Del knew what a vicious cycle revenge was, and wished with all her heart that Dana had let well enough alone. If Dana hadn't succeeded in ruining Brigid's life to avenge the humiliation she'd suffered at Ryan's hands, none of this would have happened. Leslie wouldn't have crossed party lines to back the opposition, and Del would have been celebrating tonight instead of drowning her sorrows. She swallowed the last of her drink and rose to retire for the night. Before leaving the den, she turned a mean, unhappy stare on her wife.

"I hope you're happy now. Next time, leave things alone."

The hostility in Del's words hit their mark. Dana winced and withdrew from them. She lowered her eyes guiltily and twisted her drink in her hand, wishing she had the courage to stand up to Del. Or at the very least, find a way to turn the blame on Del rather than having to accept it herself. Not so much as a civil "good night" passed between them as Del left the room.

Alone with her own thoughts, Dana found someone to share the blame with. "Well, Anara," she addressed the absent demigoddess sarcastically, "you said I would have revenge against Ryan . . ." Dana tried to stand and couldn't; she was far drunker than she'd thought. "What you didn't tell me," she slurred, "was that Ryan's little wifey would get back at me." Dana lifted her glass to animate her speech. "You, Anara, my *queen*, are a bitch." Dana's hand came down slowly to perch the nearly empty glass on the arm of the chair, but she didn't quite make it. Passing out, Dana dropped the liquid on her dress, and the glass fell to the carpet and rolled away.

January thaw: that hope-giving respite that Nature sometimes saw fit to bestow upon her Rocky Mountain region when the temperatures rose well above the seasonal norms, to the delight of all who were touched by the gift. Brigid was thankful for the springlike weather because it proved less of a shock to her system after returning from the warm beaches of France.

Suntanned and rested, Brigid was stronger, more in control, yet not able to sit at a work bench to create her ceramic art. Once before she'd needed to paint her way out of mental illness and the same cure proved as effective for her now. Of the works she'd created abroad, only two returned with her: one for her mother; the other, a seascape, sat in a corner of her shop designated as a peace offering to the O'Donnell household. The others had been purchased by a greedy art dealer, and Brigid hadn't cared.

The only thing Brigid cared about was the letter that had been forwarded to her in France. It was from Leslie: a letter of pardon. Brigid carried it with her everywhere she went; it was worn from frequent readings, over and over again as if to prove to herself that it was true, Leslie had forgiven her. But, the last line had cautioned her that Ryan had not, so she was to stay away from McKinley. The letter was Brigid's life-line; she clung to it dearly.

Why then she was driving to the high school, she couldn't say. The force that spurred her on was indescribable, intense, and more than she could resist.

Christine Latham didn't walk with a limp anymore. After being hit by a car just over a year before, she'd recovered completely in mind, body and spirit. Her cheerful and bright personality were more in evidence than they had ever been, especially since she no longer lived with or was abused by her parents. Under the guardianship of a couple who had raised six of their own children, Christine had blossomed into a stunning young woman. In the top two percent scholastically, Christine was a class officer, extremely popular, and courted by the best universities. From time to time rumors of her Lesbianism surfaced — she neither denied them or admitted their truth.

Nor did Ginny, the star of the girls soccer team whom she dated regularly. The two seventeen-year olds were walking through the school parking lot, lost in important conversation, when they were abruptly cut off by an arrogant, double-dare sportscar that missed their toes by mere inches as it came to a screeching halt in front of them.

"Hey! Watch out!" Ginny called angrily, instinctively putting up an arm to protect Christine. When the car didn't move along to let them by, Ginny let her purposeful glare alight on the driver—who was looking at her girl with more than idle admiration.

"Brigid!" Christine declared enthusiastically; she hadn't seen the redhead for several months, and was thrilled as well as surprised by her unexpected visit. The name struck a chord in Christine's date's mind: this was the cousin of the infamous Ryan O'Donnell, but, more importantly, the woman who had helped Christine through her long, painful recovery. A part of Ginny wanted to like Brigid for that. And except for Brigid's smug confidence, she would have—maybe. Ginny couldn't help admiring or envying the sleek Aston Martin Brigid was driving. There was power under that hood and refinement in the interior; its understated sexuality magnified the meaningful draw in the driver's grey eyes. Ginny, actually, had every reason to be jealous.

"Ginny, this is Brigid MacSweeney," Christine offered happily, calling attention to her companion.

Brigid's eyes swept up the athlete's body, dismissing her as not worthy of her attention. Saying nothing to Ginny and receiving nothing in reply, Brigid nodded her head toward the passenger seat of her eager-to-go car and ordered Christine, "Get in."

Excited by the invitation, Christine turned to her date. "You don't mind do you, Ginny?" It was a formality with Christine, she didn't really care if Ginny minded. "I haven't seen Brigid in ages," she added as extra ammunition.

Ginny was seething and speechless. Her teenage, macho ego had just been knocked off its pins by an older, more experienced butch with money. She would recover—smarter and none the worse for it—but for now, she stood helplessly as Christine got into Brigid's car, and the fire-red vehicle peeled out of the parking lot, drawing stares and remarks from several nearby students.

After a short time filled with high energy when neither of them spoke, Brigid finally greeted Christine. "It's good to see you again, Chris. You're looking well." Brigid approved of Christine's burgundy angora sweater dress and flats; the outfit was very becoming on a young woman with naturally rosy cheeks, *very* blue eyes and soft, flyaway blonde hair. Christine's figure was filling in nicely as was her ability to subtly call attention to it.

"My thoughts precisely. Where did you get that tan?" Christine asked enviously, noting to herself how looking debonaire seemed to run in Brigid's family. Her friend's suntan looked all the more upper crust against the grey cable-knit turtleneck and tweed slacks.

"Mother and I went on holiday in the Mediterranean," Brigid provided nonchalantly. Her thoughts were already several steps beyond the mundane. She had shifted mental gears into her seduction speed. To make way for that forward move she had to shove something backwards: the knowledge that her next move was as illegal as hell. Propelled by what-did-she-have-to-lose guts Brigid reached over and placed her large hand on Christine's knee. She scanned the traffic and looked at her passenger. "Come for a ride with me," she both requested and ordered in a low, self-assured voice. A shock of electricity flowed between them.

The feel of Brigid's inquiring, demanding hand on her knee made Christine close her eyes, briefly overcome by surprising passion. Her body tingled from the all-over feeling of excitement. The best she could do was nod her consent.

The car made an abrupt left turn, heading in a southerly direction. Brigid hadn't known where she wanted to take Christine until that moment, but now she knew that "Rich Kid's Racetrack" was the best of all possible places. Like a horse eager for its morning exercise, her Volante was ready to open up, to fulfill its V-8 destiny. Her hand was equally ready, but she held back. This situation called for the desire-building advance/welcome game similar to the one played in balconies of dark movie theaters. A game she'd played many times with a number of young ladies when she was Christine's age.

Christine's heart was beating at nearly twice its normal rhythm, and flashes of heat stormed her body, congregating in her dampening womanhood. She had never thought about sleeping with Brigid before, but when the redhead unforeseeably changed their relationship by gripping her knee, it was as though she had always known, since the first day when they shook hands on Ryan's driveway, that this would happen between them. Once she accepted that, her sensual self took charge, memorizing every aspect of this liaison: the English hide upholstery, the burled walnut, the low-slung comfort of the car.

Up to that point Brigid's hand could have withdrawn, it had not yet made the sexual commitment Christine was longing for it to make. When the sturdy palm did move off the knee and onto the thigh, taking the hem of her dress with it, Christine couldn't suppress her heart-stopping moan. Her senses formed a committee and voted to urge the hand downward. A slight shift of her weight made Brigid's palm slip closer still.

This foreplay, which they pretended wasn't going on, masterfully aroused them, sending dizzying shocks of pleasure throughout their connected bodies. Their joint quickened breathing, hardened nipples and quivering sexes ignited their nerves — all wordlessly ignored as Brigid drove on.

Once more she moved her hand closer to her goal, stealing a quick, sideways glance at Christine who was glowing with anticipation. Passing the garters now to the naked flesh of Christine's lovely thigh, Brigid let an involuntary moan escape. Christine looked Brigid's way, her own face smoothed over with longing and surrender. Brigid let her fingers nudge the other thigh, insisting, and the girl took her cue easily, moving further down into the plush seat and parting her legs.

When the car slowed to turn against the traffic, Christine dreamily checked to see where they were. She barely registered the "No Trespassing" sign they went by as they entered an open gate at the head of a seemingly endless stretch of straight-away paved before them. And just as Brigid had permission to be on that forbidden land, she had been granted the right to enter Christine's private property. She did so with ease, gliding her fingers into the silk panties, then spreading the damp lips to conquer the summit of Christine's flushed readiness.

Excitement reigned supreme. With one hand on the steering wheel, her foot on the accelerator, and her adroit middle finger on Christine's clitoris, Brigid gradually began to increase the speed of the car in harmony with the speed of her attentions to the blonde's focus of lust.

Christine was frozen in her seat, thinking of nothing but the powerful sensations wrapped around her like heat lightning: Brigid's finger touching her in just the right way, the growing growl of the hungry sportscar gorging itself on its own virility, consuming the asphalt beneath it, Brigid's harsh and quickening breath.

Never had Brigid pulled off a seduction so perfectly, with such exquisite timing, and never had she wanted a woman as she did Christine at that moment. She could almost hear her car thanking her for letting it do what it had been made to do. Her senses were acute, at their most alert, everything seemed so real and vivid. Her eyes darted along a marked path: the road ahead, the mirrors, the speedometer, Christine's face (pure ecstasy), Christine's sex (pure heaven) and back to the road. Each time she made the circuit her own passion grew, courtesy of fresh shocks of need. In her mind she was screaming impassioned cries of desire; Christine was driving her wild. But her concentration held; she said nothing to acknowledge this act.

No cars on the road, or in the mirrors . . . 90 miles per hour . . . Christine hissed . . . Brigid's finger moved more rapidly . . . the road was empty . . . the mirrors clear . . . 100 miles per hour . . . Christine moaned deeply . . . Brigid intensified her pressure . . . the road was still theirs alone . . . mirrors showed nothing (the car purred) . . . 110 miles per hour . . . Christine hissed, whimpered, her breath caught . . . Brigid jiggled her finger faster and faster (what utter power and control over woman and car) . . . no one still on the straight-stretch . . . the mirrors shimmered clearly . . . 120 miles per hour . . . Christine screamed, her body folded like a knife, her legs clamped shut on Brigid's steady hand . . . they hung suspended for a few glorious seconds as the car nearly lifted from the pavement while Christine was dashed senseless by the most severe orgasm she had ever felt.

Brigid brought Christine down carefully, decreasing her speed in stages until they were twenty miles from where they'd begun. They had reached the end of the private playground for expensive sportscar owners. Brigid turned the wheel abruptly, pulled her hand from Christine's sex and floored the car. There was no need to tell her guest where they were going at top speed or why Brigid needed every bit of her will power to get them to the carriage house in the shortest possible time. Christine knew. She sat back and reveled in the thrill of the race and the intoxication of being needed *that* badly.

Christine was fascinated by how deftly Brigid brought the car to a sliding halt in her driveway, got herself and her crutches out of the vehicle and was on her side opening the door. She was enjoying Brigid's necessitous behavior—a call for coyness if ever there was one. Calmly she moved one leg out, forcing her dress to ride up her thigh sharpening Brigid's lecherous expression. She took the proffered hand daintily and glided gracefully out of her seat, then walked serenely to Brigid's front door. Brigid opened it hastily and waited for her guest to go in, now barely able to control her actions.

If she had been thinking beyond each exasperating moment, she would have entered first to keep Christine from noticing the portrait that was in progress on her easel. But it was the first thing to catch the young woman's eyes, and she walked over to it, momentarily captivated. The last thing Brigid wanted was to remind Christine of her past love affair with Ryan.

"When did you . . .?" Christine began to ask. She was cut off harshly.

Brigid's eyes grew large and intense, her voice imperative. "*Later*, Christine," she advised while grabbing the girl by the upper arm and turning her toward the stairs to her living quarters.

"Oh," Christine said like a child who had been distracted by a new toy to keep it from trouble. "All right," she added to infuriate the redhead, then scampered up the stairs, followed closely by her relentless pursuer.

Once on the second level, Christine ignored her surroundings and turned her attention to Brigid, backing the older woman up to the edge of her bed, locking eyes with her.

Looking down from her six-foot vantage point at this girl— woman turned enchantress, it was hard for Brigid not to let her eyes speak for her—pleading, urging, demanding, whatever it took to get this child to make love to her.

Without lowering her eyes from Brigid's, Christine unfastened the redhead's belt and unzipped her trousers. Teasingly, she nudged the garment over the naked hips letting the weight of the car keys and wallet do the rest of her work for her. The slacks fell to the floor with a chink and a bump leaving the Irishwoman exposed and frantic.

During Christine's long hospital stay and even longer physical therapy she had grown completely comfortable in the company of the physically impaired. Brigid's stump neither repulsed or attracted her. It was simply another part of Brigid, like her freckles or her art, and Christine accepted it as such. She encouraged her objective to sit on the bed while she took off the dress slip-on shoe and ribbed sock; the slacks came the rest of the way off. Brigid placed her crutches against the wall impatiently and seized the temptress, pulling her onto the bed where she could make her need more pointedly known. But Christine wasn't cooperative, she wanted to be asked, begged if need be.

Finally Brigid couldn't take it any more. Propped up on one elbow, her free hand guided Christine's head downward to her drenched, vibrating sex. Her voice was hoarse as she panted, "*Jesus* god, Chris, help me out here."

"Ohh," Christine moaned. She could take no more of this protracted desire either. She gave no resistance to the strong hand urgently moving her head into place. Her first kiss on the fine, red mass of sex hair unlocked a deeper set of needs in both women. Christine had never wanted to please anyone the way she wanted to please Brigid. She had had occasional partners who had asked her to make oral love to them, but it had always seemed like play. This was the real thing for Christine, and she wanted it desperately. Her tongue circled and dove, flicked and penetrated in accord with Brigid's hisses and moans.

As Brigid neared fulfillment she gasped out a final instruction before losing herself to incoherent carnal delight, "Lick it like an ice cream cone, baby!"

Gladly, Christine thought to herself as she performed as bidden, relishing every stroke over Brigid's stiff and tense clitoris, her tongue flat and pliable, moist and maddening, gliding slowly, then returning to glide again, and again.

"Oh god, oh god," Brigid's cries mounted, "oh, yes, oh, Chris, ohhh, hssss." Brigid held her breath for three more ecstatic strokes then folded into howling contractions that devastated her entire system.

Now nothing was more important to Brigid than having Christine in her arms to hold close and know the supreme contentment of the moment. Brigid hadn't planned to feel anything beyond sexual conquest in this encounter. She lingered on the verge of their first kiss, trying to talk herself out of going through with it, but her battle against emotional involvement was not well fought. The buds of new love were swelling inside her and, if she hadn't seen the signs of similar stirrings in Christine's eyes, she would have turned back. Softly, with a slow, fog-filtered approach to her future, Brigid brought Christine's sweet lips to her own. The kiss lasted for long, enchanting moments, ending with the bittersweet reluctance that accompanies such kisses between those born for each other.

"Stay for dinner with me," Brigid suggested desirously.

Christine looked at her watch and realized it was nearly dark. Brigid reached for the lamp on her bedside table and turned it on for her. Christine sighed with disappointment. "I can't, Brig. It's late and I have homework to do. The Sorensons will be wondering where I am before long," she explained, knowing that her foster family would have dinner waiting for her.

"They take good care of you," Brigid half asked to reassure herself that all was well for this precious woman she was holding more dear by the moment.

"They do," Christine verified, placing her hand on Brigid's arm with a tender gesture of affection. She was surprised with herself. After being forcibly separated from Ryan she had vowed never to allow herself to care for another woman. But it seemed so natural with Brigid, she trusted the feeling and didn't hide from it.

Brigid gritted her teeth when she saw the ring on Christine's fragile finger. It was the one thing she had hoped she wouldn't see even though the gift from her cousin had been as instrumental in saving Christine's life after her accident as Leslie's letter was in keeping her hanging on to her own life.

"But," Christine chirped, suddenly aware that Brigid had noticed the ring, "could you come to my madrigal practice tonight?" Her eyes were bright and hopeful.

"I'd like that," Brigid admitted sincerely.

"Great! Eight o'clock in the choir room. Oh . . ." Christine remembered that Brigid had attended a school for the gifted and probably didn't know her way around her high school.

Brigid smiled, intuiting Christine's discomfort. "I'll find it."

Christine's smile was warm and mature. "Thank you. I really have to go now. I don't want to."

"Nor do I want you to. But we can't raise any storm clouds on the home front." Brigid didn't need to say it out loud that Christine wasn't old enough to be dating her.

On their way out of the carriage house, Christine stopped to inspect the portrait Brigid had been working on. It was of Ryan wearing morning wear which fascinated Christine tremendously. Then she spied the photograph Brigid was using as a guide, and a question formed in her mind. Something didn't seem right about all this. It was unlikely that Ryan would have sat for a portrait anyway, especially not in formal daytime attire. Even still . . .

"Who took this picture?" she asked, knowing from the greying temples under the top hat that it was recent.

"My mother. It was Leslie's idea . . ." Brigid's voice trailed off regretfully. That Ryan had married another woman was something Christine had not yet accepted, and mentioning it now wasn't wise.

Christine ignored the comment as she ignored Leslie's existence. "Why isn't Ryan sitting for you?"

This was not the time to explain family problems and Brigid dodged the question. "Aren't you going to be late for dinner?"

"Probably,"Christine answered idly as she put the photo back and let herself be escorted out the door.

7

"How could I have been so stupid?" Anara paced agitatedly up and down the length of her bedchamber cursing herself for acting foolishly about Blaise. It had been her intention to keep her fiery consort safe in an ignorant state of complacency, under her control until it was too late to fight the battle for The Throne of Council — unaware that co-ruling The Throne meant Anara ruled while Blaise watched and slavishly adored Anara.

Anara's handmaiden, Fila, stood at attention near the foot of Anara's tremendous bed: legs apart, arms folded across her chest, eyes following carefully, confidently, every movement of her Mistress' exciting body. She could afford to be confident now; Anara's rage was nearly spent although the dying embers of it could be detected in the rims of her arresting white eyes. She knew Anara was done with making her pay for a crime she did not commit. The bruises would fade, the slashes would seal over, the pain of being the brunt of Anara's anger with herself for overlooking the tiny detail of setting Brigid up to force herself on Leslie thus bringing Blaise to her senses and ending her misguided love affair with Anara would go away. Fila wasn't thinking about any of that now. While her heavily muscled, expertly trained, bronze, glistening body was sturdily rigid and poised, her eyes stayed with the object of her need.

Gesticulating, swearing, traversing the path of her self-reproach, Anara was unconcerned that her breasts were swaying and bobbing under her amethyst chiffon shift. It didn't occur to her that her long, purposeful strides accentuated her back and backside or that her flowing ebony hair caught the muted light and threw it back as flashes of sapphire. She didn't know until she caught sight of it out of the corner of her eye as she threw herself, face down, on her bed that she had worked Fila into a fever. By the time her breasts made contact with the plush bedcovers her nipples were taut. In that short second Anara had seen and responded to the glassy sheen of excitement that swelled over Fila's eyes when she craved Anara's responsive body. And the film of sweat that made Fila's muscles seem to bulge and flex even when she was still, was a sight that took Anara by surprise and made her instantly ready.

Blaise had been a good lover—submissive, obedient, willing—but Fila had power, strength, imagination, uncontrollable passion. Anara thrived on her handmaiden's animalistic intensity; she missed it and wanted it, now. Shivering with anticipation, she waited to see how Fila would return to her.

There was no doubt whatsoever in Fila's mind just how she would take her Mistress, and there was no time to waste—it had been far too long. She had eyes for one thing and one thing alone: Anara's inviting backside. She glided onto the bed with the stealth of a trained soldier, moving the sheer fabric out of her way as she made her direct approach.

Anara hissed, relaxed, floated on the surface of her own steam when she felt Fila's massive hands part her buttocks to make way for an impatient tongue. Anara knew Fila wanted to make her weak (and there was no better way to do so) to restore her sense of virility, rebuild the image so recently torn down by undeserved abuse. Fila needed to overpower Anara and remember how incredibly easy a thing that was to do.

Softly, slowly, she licked the area around Anara's all too responsive back entrance. Her forceful fingers kneaded the white mounds, pulling them further apart, digging painfully into them as she took aim at the pink, tense target with the arrow of her tongue. One deep thrust inside and Anara was hers—unguarded, vulnerable, desperate.

Anara hissed into and clenched her pillow, gritting her teeth against the initial pain, then went under. Went under for this massive amazon, went under for the sheer poignancy and deliciousness of being mastered by her slave. This one act Anara could *not* resist.

"*Fiiilllaaa, ohhhh,*" Anara whispered helplessly. It was only a matter of time before she would be wailing, pleading, begging for this beast of prey to take her, use her, reduce her to a feeble heap of satisfied spirit-flesh.

This was something Fila knew only too well, and she drew it out for as long as she, herself, could bear, for her own passion was unbridled and set free to run with the winds when she set upon her Mistress from behind.

"Ooohmm." Fila's deep, barreling moans were equal to any thunderstorm conjured by the gods at play in their boiling clouds. The more Anara pleaded the deeper Fila buried her face into the musky hole, the faster she jerked back and forth lost in her mindless ecstasy.

Anara couldn't handle it any more. She had to attain satisfaction, even at the cost of begging. "Fila!" she screamed. "Take me, please. *PLEASE!* I can't stand it. Fila . . . oh, do it. Do it, take me. Ohhhh."

"Beg me!" Fila managed to demand through her insanity. Her hand would go nowhere until Anara was reduced to tears, until her body wrenched and heaved, her fingers clawed and scratched, until the final limit was met and surpassed.

Fila wouldn't trade the sight before her for all the power in the Universe: Anara — delirious, crying fitfully, begging with all her might — reduced. One tiny moment beyond Anara's endurance and then Fila took her Mistress, her queen. One hand grabbed Anara's tight abdomen for support while she forced her thick thumb into the dark, open womb. Simultaneously her masterful bow fingers flanked Anara's hardened clitoris and *took . . . everything . . . Anara . . . had.*

Between the quickly thrusting tongue, jabbing thumb, fingers massaging at breakneck speed, Anara knew nothing, felt beyond everything, and crashed into unconsciousness as she was robbed of her sexual prowess and overtaken by her stellar climax.

Undeterred by the limp, indifferent body left to her, Fila ripped her digits from it and fell upon it to take her own satisfaction. Her wide pelvis eclipsed the ravaged backside as she mounted and rode the unmoving woman until she dove off her own cliff into the dark abyss of gratification and exhaustion.

The aftermath of their lovemaking found Anara resting quietly in Fila's arms listening to her amazon's steady breath of sleep and thinking, plotting. She was relaxed now, her mind clear and focused; she could see her way through the battle to The Throne and was smiling — evil and content.

"Dove, I don't think it's going to be an issue," Ryan insisted gently, addressing her wife with her favorite term of endearment. Leslie was lying on her side, Ryan's head resting on her thighs. Coffee cups, papers, empty champagne glasses and half-filled ashtrays were sprawled on the bed as the lovers were: lazily and as if they had always been there.

Leslie kissed the end of Ryan's black robe sash, then put her head on her lover's legs. "These are young ladies we're talking about here. You don't think our sexual preferences will offend their sensibilities? They're going to be living just down the hall — what are we to have them told? 'Ignore those screams, girls, Sanji's just happy.'?" Leslie lifted a teasing eyebrow in a manner that elicited a devious wink from Ryan.

"Why not?" Ryan asked sincerely. "Most artists would sell their soul to have a patron for their work. If a young student is going to attend this art institute," she motioned toward the papers spread around them to indicate the many plans that were in the development stages, "then she is going to have to look the other way when it comes to her patron's eccentricities." Ryan's words sounded more like a pronouncement than friendly discussion.

Leslie suppressed a giggle and pressed on. "So, part of the admittance criteria is . . ." Leslie's smile tightened against the laughter in her throat, "that if she makes it through the final selection process," Leslie couldn't prevent the tiny chuckle that punctuated her idea, "she'll be taken aside and discreetly informed . . . oh, Ryan," she giggled, "that she must look the other way?" Leslie couldn't finish; her sweet laughter filled the vast bedroom and infected her mate.

Together they could feature the scene, mentally supplying either of the two women who headed the selection committee — Brigid's mother, Aisling, or Marguarita, an art dealer they worked closely with — seeing one of them pulling aside a college-age applicant to inform her that if she were accepted into the program she would have to ignore what went on around her.

Leslie continued to paint the picture. "I can just see Aisling saying, 'Now, dear, there are certain things that go on at McKinley you simply must overlook'." Leslie mocked Aisling's maternal voice and broke out in peals of laughter.

Once the mirth calmed, Leslie noticed the fleeting vacant look on Ryan's restful face that pointed to thoughts of Brigid, as was often the case when they talked of founding an institute to patronize and teach promising young women with likely careers in the fine arts. Leslie ran her hand softly over her lover's cheek while her eyes begged her yet one more time to forgive her cousin. But Ryan remained unresponsive and stubbornly unforgiving. Even still, they both knew that Ryan couldn't find her center, get her life in order, until she found it in her heart to let her hatred of her cousin go.

Instead, Ryan dodged the problem by taking advantage of her body being lined up in the opposite direction as her wife's. Her knowing hand opened Leslie's silk robe and pulled her lover's torso onto her own, spread Leslie's legs and sex lips to give what she herself was in need of. Leslie, every-ready to kiss Ryan's sex, didn't object in the least. As one, they gave and received the other's gift of love and lust — to fulfillment.

Brigid was happy. The time she had been spending with Christine had begun to heal some of her piercing wounds. The young woman was sunshine breaking through Brigid's clouds of depression and grief. The love they were building was beginning to show in Brigid's artwork which had proliferated in the five weeks since she and Christine had become lovers. Christine's guardians encouraged the relationship rather than cause her any difficulty which might interfere with *her* healing process. All anyone had to do was look to see how much Christine had grown to love Brigid in return.

From the mid-February chill the couple brought their warmth and affection to a dimly lighted, Seventeenth Avenue restaurant for a quiet dinner. Approving of the seafood appetizer, Brigid was nodding to the waiter when her eyes were drawn to a darker part of the dining room and a jolting sight: Dana Schaeffer, sitting alone.

Brigid's astonished expression drew Christine's attention to the near-mirage (for one was never quite certain one actually *saw* Dana) and she knew her instantly for the woman in one of Brigid's paintings in the corner of her shop. "She's just as beautiful in person," Christine commented with amazement. Somehow she hadn't expected Dana to be quite so attractive. Why not, Chris? she asked herself. You know the scuttlebutt as well as anyone — better. She *was* Ryan's first wife, came her mental reminder. Brigid loved her once, too. Is it so odd that she should be absolutely *gorgeous*? Christine refused to feel even the slightest jealousy toward Dana despite the fact that Brigid had just excused herself to go talk to the "Bitch", Christine whispered under her breath, then corrected herself quickly. Like Ryan, Brigid would not tolerate any schoolgirl cattiness or petty, unladylike behavior. Deftly she realigned her attitude and greeted the woman, who had just been invited to their table, with cool, polite detachment.

"Dana Schaeffer, this is Christine Latham. Christine Latham, Miss Dana Schaeffer. Chris, I've invited Dana to join us. Del is out of town," Brigid inserted more to reassure herself that she was safe from Dana's lover's temper than to explain the situation to her own lover. It was common knowledge that Del had threatened to kill Brigid if she ever came near Dana again. Brigid was acting on her emotions instead of her reason, but she wasn't the first woman who couldn't think sensibly around Dana.

Fortunately for Christine and irritably for Dana, Christine was immune to Dana's charms. "How do you do?" Christine extended her hand to take Dana's rather gingerly and with no desire to mask her dislike of the new dinner guest. It amazed Christine that Brigid didn't seem to notice how drunk Dana was.

"Charmed, I'm sure," Dana retorted handily. The whole exchange was rife with masked distaste and contempt, and obscured from the normally observant, sensitive artist sitting between them.

Dana sized up Brigid's date easily. So this is the little thing Ryan went to so much trouble for, she thought meanly. In love with Brig, eh? And *fighting* to keep from being jealous of me. Ha. Not with Brigid over here making a fool of herself about me. Take notes, darling, Dana wanted to tell Christine, you might learn something.

Even falling-down-drunk Dana was a master of seduction. "My goodness it's warm in here," Dana announced as she peeled off her sequined jacket and let it drape over her chairback. Brigid swallowed hard at the sight of Dana's black crepe dress: rhinestone spaghetti straps on a dangerously low-cut bodice and fitting so tightly that Dana's every breath was accentuated and highlighted.

Christine went from wondering how Dana was going to keep from popping out of her dress to wondering how Brigid's eyes were going to keep from popping out of her head.

"Brig, dear, I hear you were ill last year," Dana prodded, knowing Brigid wouldn't want to talk about how she had gone mad for a time after breaking up with her lover, Star, and having her heart broken by Dana herself.

Brigid stirred her onion soup with a breadstick, avoiding Dana's eyes. "You know I was, Dana. I'm fine now."

"I see. It must have been awfully nice staying at McKinley, being fussed and fawned over by Ryan's household . . . including her . . . wife."

To Christine: "Ryan was ill, too, you know," Dana went on. "Or hasn't anyone told you that whenever Brigid is in pain or is ill, Ryan suffers a similar fate?" Dana's cruelty knew no bounds; she took delight in making Christine singularly uncomfortable.

Christine shifted nervously in her chair and sent a 'what-is-she-driving-at' look Brigid's way. Brigid's eyes answered: I don't know, but whatever it is, I don't like it.

"From what I hear, Brigid, you took rather too kindly to Leslie's attentions. She was just trying to help, you know."

"Shut up, Dana," Brigid threatened.

"Don't be impolite, Brig," Dana chastised. She turned her meanness back on Christine. "My dear, you look puzzled. Certainly Brig told you that Ryan and she are no longer on speaking terms."

Christine turned suddenly to Brigid for confirmation but had to settle for the deadly look her lover was casting on their now very unwanted guest. Brigid hadn't told her of the rift between herself and Ryan. Nor had she said anything to indicate that Leslie had meant anything to her beyond friendship.

"No, I see she hasn't," Dana continued as she extracted her wrist from Brigid's warning grip. Brigid bent over to get her crutches; she was preparing to leave; she had had enough of this. It was the venom in Dana's voice that tipped her off, that opened the doors of befuddled pain and let in the truth.

"Hasn't told you that she fell in love with Leslie and that she . . . raped . . . her?"

Christine's fork fell noisily to her plate, her mouth opened in astonishment; she was speechless. Brigid's face was a mirror of her lover's: wide-eyed and stunned, but for a different reason. It didn't surprise her that Dana was vicious enough to lay this trap, or cold-blooded enough to make Christine yet another victim of her twisted malevolence. What shocked her was finally seeing what really had happened.

"You *planned* it," Brigid breathed incredulously. "Everything. The illicit love affair, Star leaving, you denying to Del that you knew I loved you. You *knew* I'd go off the deep end, that Ryan would suffer, that I'd get too close to Leslie, that I'd force myself on her, that Ryan would end up hating me," Brigid recounted the series of tragedies with fascination. "Why, Dana? What did I ever do to you?" Brigid pleaded for enlightenment.

Dana was beyond the glee of the moment, her liquor was her master now. She had never really planned to tell Brigid about her motivations, but she was loose-mouthed and had sunk to the depths of her hatred for Ryan.

"You fool," Dana spat. "Did you think you were so important that I'd want to hurt *you*?"

It was all laid out before Brigid now — clear and almost beautiful in its cold, calculating purity — Dana's plan. The truth was the scalpel cutting out the last cancerous cell of love Brigid had ever felt for Dana. "God, Dana. You don't care about anyone, do you?"

Christine listened and watched as Brigid became transformed before her. She had all but forgotten about their guest. She was not appalled, as Dana had hoped she would be, but filled with compassion for Brigid and all Brigid had been through.

The redhead's eyes were filled with hatred. "You broke my heart, made me break Star's, ended my friendship with Del, made Ryan take on all my pain, made Leslie suffer immeasurably . . . then wadded it all up in a ball and just now threw it in Christine's face. All that to get back at Ryan for hurting and humiliating you. You are the lowest form of life, Dana." Brigid pulled herself up taller than she'd stood in over a year. "Chris, we're going. I'll explain everything to you on the way back to your home." She ushered Christine out of the dining room — away from the death that had been taking her, slowly and pitilessly — to the life that she knew she deserved to live.

8

The logs in the fireplace hissed and popped from the resin of the starter pine. Brigid eased too large oak logs into place and put the screen back to shield them from sparks. Christine's guardians, the Sorensons, were away for the weekend leaving the two lovers alone with a small live-in staff who were careful not to interrupt their goings on. Brigid had stolen two or three furtive glances at the young woman stretched out on the plush wool rug in front of the fireplace. She couldn't bring herself to stare openly while Christine read the dilapidated letter Brigid had shown her; she was too worried about the outcome, too concerned that this seventeen-year-old might not understand what had gone on. Brigid could have throttled Dana for telling Christine about how she had violated Leslie (how Dana knew about it was a mystery to Brigid). But the telling was done, and in a way Brigid was glad to have it over with. When she looked at Christine again, the girl was patting the floor beside her, encouraging the redhead to join her on the rug.

Leslie had never seemed real to Christine until she read the letter Brigid had shown her. She'd seen the woman's picture, knew but refused to accept that Leslie had captured Ryan's heart for all time, but until this moment she had been just a name, a thorn in Christine's side. Learning about the rape, hearing Brigid's account of it and seeing how Leslie had so sweetly and sincerely forgiven Brigid brought her to life for Christine. But even more, it made her respect this woman whom she could now acknowledge and wished to meet.

Taking Brigid's hand tenderly, Christine spoke knowingly. "Leslie's forgiven you, Brig, and she means it. She understands you and what drove you to such drastic measures. So do I," she reassured firmly.

"Do you?" Brigid's eyes searched for further confirmation.

"Yes, I do. You weren't yourself when you did this to her. In the time we've spent together I've come to know that you have the gentlest of hearts, but one that is trapped in a wild spirit. You were being manipulated and used by those more powerful than you . . ." Christine's voice trailed off; she looked toward the rug letting her finger trail over the floral design in the weave.

"And?" Brigid took Christine's pretty chin in her hand bringing the youth's blue eyes level with her own grey ones—questioning.

"And . . . I wish Ryan would forgive you also," Christine added sadly.

Brigid sighed heavily and withdrew into herself. Ryan was standing in the way of her happiness in more than one area of her life.

"Don't go away from me, Brig. Whatever it is that is bothering you, I want to share it." Christine squeezed Brigid's large hand with her own tiny one to keep the connection between them intact. She was not going to let her lover sink into thoughtful depression.

"It's the *ring*, Chris," Brigid stated resentfully.

Christine pulled her hand away suddenly. Being protective of the ring Ryan had given her when she was fifteen was a habit with her. It had been taken away from her once before and she had nearly died in an effort to seek comfort from Ryan because of it. The ring's presence on her finger symbolized her lifeline to the only love she had ever really known.

Brigid knew all that and sympathized with the girl, but now Christine had love, tangible love, and holding on to her loyalty to Ryan and the notion of that pure, albeit no longer existent, bond was preventing her from making a stronger commitment to Brigid. "Christine, I love you. I know this is right for us. But our relationship can best be served if you keep the ring in your jewelry case instead of on your finger." Brigid worked to keep

90

her words warm and compassionate, not overbearing or demanding.

Christine toyed with the diamond and gold wedding band that had once belonged to Ryan's mother. Her thoughts were filled with bittersweet memories, cherished moments, leftover longings. "I loved her so, Brig," Christine began to weep quietly.

"I know you did, baby. She loved you, too. You were there when she needed you, with all your precious purity. She's married now, and happy. I know she would want this for you, Chris. I *need* to stop competing with her memory. I need you to be with me, completely. Do this for me, for us," Brigid appealed.

Unsteadily, Christine removed the band from her finger. When the deed was done, she cried even more, all the time being comforted steadfastly in Brigid's strong arms.

In time, Christine relaxed, the release complete and done with. Brigid reached behind her and felt for the pocket of her bulky overcoat taking from it a small velvet case. "Wear this instead, my love." She handed it to her lover and smiled.

Christine dried her eyes and turned a quizzical gaze up to Brigid.

"Go ahead, open it." Brigid prompted.

Christine did and gasped at the sight of a star sapphire suspended over a thin ring of solid yellow gold. "*Brigid . . .* it's beautiful!"

"I designed it for you, darling: blue for your eyes and gold for your hair." Brigid was very pleased that the goldsmith had done justice to her simple, delicate design. She took the golden circle from the case and slipped it on the finger where Ryan's ring had been. The fit was as perfect as the look of the ring and the expression of awe and delight on her lover's face.

"For *me*? You had this made for me?!" Christine was absolutely dazed. No one had ever done anything so special just for her. "Oh, Brigid," she whispered, "I can't tell you how wonderful this makes me feel." Christine was so absorbed in looking at the ring that she didn't notice that Brigid had already unbuttoned her blouse and was unfastening the front hook of her bra.

"Show me how good . . . it . . . feels," Brigid demanded passionately.

"Oh, Brig, I love you so much." Christine's whole body glowed in the firelight, drawing Brigid into it.

"I want you, young lady." Brigid had intended to wait, to take her time making love to this morsel of a girl, but she couldn't hold back any longer.

Christine took in the sight of Brigid's large hand exploring her firm breast. Next to this Irishwoman's undiluted desire, it was Brigid's broad, virile hands that stirred Christine in the deep recesses of her woman's nature. The striking contrast between coarse, indelicate appearance of the hands and the masterful dexterity they possessed set her imagination in motion. The double stimulus of *seeing* these great hands caressing her, calling to mind romanticized debaucheries of young maids, and *feeling* the knowing artistry that guided these provocative palms and fingers about her body kept Christine fully involved in what was happening to her mind and body. Thus engaged, she remained fully open to her lover's rapt attentions.

Another of Brigid's winning attributes was her mouth. Strong yet gentle, the pliant lips surrounded the pert tip of Christine's nipple while the tongue danced about on the flat surface of excited nerve endings. Sighing in waves, Christine shivered and squirmed; her need mounted. She herself guided the expert hand downward, hastening the inevitable. "Hsss, ohh," she cried sweetly when the well-versed middle finger moved inside her. "Brig, I'm so ready for you," Christine panted. "Please don't make me wait." Patience is not always attainable by the young. Or the passionate — Brigid silently focused her narrowed eyes on her now desperate lover's pleading face. She smiled cockily as she nonchalantly ravished her date's sex with her finger until the girl moved through her orgasm into chest-heaving gratitude and finally into childish cuddling that brought about soft sleep.

Ryan had spent the night talking with Leslie, and pacing in her den, trying to see her way clear to forgive her cousin. It had been Leslie's suggestion that she measure three decades of intimate friendship against this one passionate, violent injury that was making Ryan overcome her unreasonable stubbornness. Her position had been rendered untenable from the moment Leslie had shown true compassion by forgiving Brigid, for it was Leslie who was the injured party and not Ryan. It had been pure Irish obduracy and pride that had kept Ryan at odds with her cousin, a woman with whom she had been extremely close since early childhood.

But, at last, the scales had come down on Brigid's side and Ryan was navigating her motorcycle against a strong March wind toward Brigid's home. She welcomed the turn into Sage Gulch as she passed the evergreen windbreak and rode along the quiet drive to Brigid's carriage house. The Aston Martin was nowhere in sight but Ryan was unconcerned as she yanked her massive motorcycle onto its kickstand and dismounted.

Ryan smiled when she tried the front door and it yielded to her. The artist had yet to be convinced that locking her door was an essential part of city life — Brigid simply never felt unsafe either about her person or her art (which by now, as Ryan looked about the workshop where she stood appraising each piece with her trained eye, could easily be valued in excess of a half a million dollars).

When her eyes alighted on the nearly finished portrait of Christine, she whistled under her breath. She found it reassuring the sudden recall that her higher self had contributed to the making of this relationship between her cousin and the pure and delightful blonde captured on the canvas before her. Brigid needed to have someone to shower with love and affection — and Christine deserved to be the beneficiary of Brigid's large and generous heart. Ryan was glad she had come, certain now that she was doing the right thing. She lit a cigarette and settled in a chair to wait for Brigid, and to admire the portrait to its memory-stimulating fullest extent.

Brigid spotted the dark figure of Ryan's motorcycle from far off; her heart was in her throat when she parked her sportscar next to it. She knew her cousin well enough to know that there could only be one reason for her visit, and Brigid was choked with happiness. Quietly, she walked in and took a seat on her bench opposite her visitor. Her pulse raced but she said nothing; just sat unmoving, waiting, and searching the depths of the jade eyes that spoke volumes of love and forgiveness.

"Chris has become a beautiful young woman," Ryan commented to close the distance between them.

"I love her, Ryan," Brigid answered defensively.

Ryan was quick to put the redhead at ease by countering with firm support. "I can see that. Your work shows every bit of it. I couldn't be happier for you, or Chris. You'll be good for one another, it's clear. I know Leslie will be excited when she learns of it. How are the Sorensons behaving toward you?"

Brigid relaxed and leaned against her work table, entering into intimate conversation with Ryan as though they had never been apart. "They've taken a "hands off" attitude. I'm not sure if they think this is a phase Chris is going through or what, but they are careful not to interfere with her emotional life. They are so proud of her for her work at school that they are willing to overlook this. Chris graduates this May," Brigid added pridefully. "She wants to go to D.U. for a business degree."

"She must be excited about leaving high school early. I'm proud of her."

"How are things between you and Leslie?" Brigid asked seriously.

Ryan nodded her head positively, approving of her own situation. "Quite well, quite well. I've gotten a handle on my drinking . . . I'm flying again . . . I spend the rest of my time with Leslie . . ." Ryan trailed off her conversation pensively. "She misses you, Brig." Ryan couldn't say, "I do, too." It was too awkward a thing for her to express.

Brigid was glad that Ryan and Leslie were together again. Their past unhappiness weighed heavily on her heart. "I'm relieved and happy that you're on course again." Brigid couldn't say she missed Ryan and Leslie either. What she needed to hear was that this ordeal was truly over. "Do you forgive me?" she asked cautiously.

Ryan had finally and genuinely learned how to forgive in her heart. "Yes," she answered simply, then stood to offer her handshake to her friend. After a sound clap on Brigid's broad shoulder she brightened with relief. This encounter hadn't been as difficult as she had feared it might. "Bring Chris for dinner this Friday. I want her to meet Leslie. And you and I have some things to discuss about an art institute that is in the works. Eight o'clock," Ryan clarified confidently. She was at peace, herself, and glad of it.

Brigid smiled. "We'll be there, Ryan," she confirmed with the smoothness she was accustomed to using to answer one of Ryan's imperious invitations. Her heart was flying with the eagles as Ryan walked out the door and rode calmly away on her motorcycle.

9

The housekeeper, Bonnie, greeted the dinner guests at the front door with enthusiasm and warmth. "Brigid, lass, come in! 'Tis grand to see ye again, and lookin' so well."

"Thank you, Bonnie. You remember Miss Latham," Brigid replied as she encouraged Christine to step forward. If anyone could help Christine overcome a feeling of intimidation by the grandeur of McKinley, it was Bonnie with her good-natured openness and earthbound manner.

"Aye," Bonnie declared, "indeed I do. My how you've grown, child," Bonnie appraised. "Last I saw ye, ye were nothing but a mere slip of a girl, and now look at ye — a full-grown woman ye are. And a pretty one, too." A person would be hard pressed not to like Christine. Bonnie had more reason to like her than others because she knew how instrumental the girl had been in helping Ryan back to health when she needed it most. Seeing that Christine was relaxing, Bonnie led the couple to the sitting room. "They're in here having tea and sherry, and asked that ye join them."

The opening of the sitting room doors found Leslie pouring herself a second glass of sherry. She set the glass and decanter down and walked over to meet their guests. Ryan stood politely, hanging back until Brigid felt comfortably welcomed.

"Brigid, welcome. I'm so glad you're here." Leslie made the

first move by giving her tall friend a firm, loving hug. Christine was quiet, waiting patiently while Leslie let Brigid know that she was truly forgiven. Hesitantly Brigid placed her arms around her hostess, then gave way to the feeling of goodness and sincerity in Leslie's heart. She returned the hug with meaning and allowed the catharsis to work its magic. At length Brigid was able to whisper a gentle "thank you" and let go of Leslie.

Again Leslie acted first by dispensing with tedious formal introductions. She extended her hand to Brigid's lover. "You must be Christine. Welcome to McKinley. We're happy you could join us. I'm Leslie." She wanted the relationship on a first name basis from the beginning—Christine was as close to family as one could be to Ryan and Leslie; it was important for the young woman to feel that way.

Christine took this stunningly sophisticated woman's hand in hers, feeling the controlled power in the firm grip. It was at once clear why Ryan had needed and chosen this person for her wife—here was someone who could meet Ryan's level of sophistication and intensity. Christine admired Leslie instantly. "How do you do? Thank you for having us."

Leslie smiled. Christine had a lot of potential for becoming a gracious, charming adult. "May I get some tea for you, or sherry perhaps?"

"I'm a little nervous," Christine admitted.

"Ah, this tea will be good for you then. It relaxes the nerves and calms the stomach. Brigid?" Leslie turned to her friend who she knew wouldn't drink sherry, but could use the nervine tea as much as her lover.

"Tea would be fine, thank you."

"Ryan?" Leslie inquired casually, drawing everyone's attention toward her as she withdrew to the serving cart.

"I'm fine," Ryan answered absently. She had been staring at Christine since she walked into the room, making no effort to come forward. One thing she liked about Christine was that she never tried to look older than she was. Her only makeup was a pale shade of pink lipstick that matched her angora dress which was complimented by a single strand of pearls and low heels. Very nice.

"Hello, Chris." Ryan's voice was deepened by the slightest trace of passion, but it rang true to confidence and detachment.

Her affair with this girl was over although a part of her heart had Christine's name on it.

Christine had never seen Ryan wearing anything other than denim and leather before. This sobering sight of her dressed in a dinner jacket and slacks brought home the reality that Ryan was an idealized memory she held sacred in her heart. Who Ryan really was — the sophisticated, debonaire Irishwoman with unmentionable wealth and a unique destiny — was someone who needed a woman of Leslie's caliber, not a youth of seventeen who had so much yet to learn about life and love.

"Hello, Ryan," Christine was able to return with poise. But for all her composure, Christine's hand sought out Brigid's for comfort.

"Won't you sit down?" Ryan invited, motioning to the two chairs nearest her own and Leslie's.

The guests took their tea and sat down together, but it was Brigid and Leslie who found themselves watching Ryan and Christine for signs that the affair was, beyond all doubt, over.

"I hear you're doing well in school, Chris. I'm proud of you. Have you been accepted to D.U. yet?"

"I have," Christine answered cheerfully. She was looking forward to attending the University.

"Fine school. Leslie did her undergraduate and Law studies there." Ryan touched her wife's arm with a fond gesture that spelled intimacy and love.

Leslie relaxed. It was clear Ryan was feeling like a protective friend toward their young guest. It was then that she noticed the ring on Christine's finger. "Chris-tine! What a lovely ring," Leslie exclaimed with appreciation.

"Thank you." Christine brought her hand out where Leslie could inspect the jewel more closely. Ryan leaned over to admire it also. "Brigid designed it for me," Christine told them with all the joy and pride a teenager was capable of expressing, which was considerable.

"Well, congratulations are in order all the way around. We're very happy for you, dear. And you, Brig," Leslie added with pleasure. Although not recognized by society at large, among the four women present the ring clearly symbolized an engagement of sorts — the beginning of a commitment made between these two lovers to make a life together and share the joys as well as the trials in store for them. The lovers gazed at one another for some time, looking every bit as though they might not return to normal conversation.

Leslie cleared her throat softly and spoke. "I believe dinner is ready if you are."

"Hmm? Oh, yes, please. We're ready," Brigid agreed hungrily. Good food and McKinley were synonymous.

Before leaving the sitting room Christine approached Ryan. "Ryan, I never got the opportunity to thank you for making it possible for me to live with the Sorensons. They've been very kind to me."

"I was glad I could help, Chris. You would have done the same for a friend if you could. You're happy, that's what counts. I think what you need now is a good hot meal. Shall we?" Ryan didn't like to draw attention to her generosity. Silently she made way for the ladies to enter the hall; when Brigid walked by her she laid her hand on her cousin's shoulder and nodded wordlessly to give further assurance that Brigid had nothing to worry about from either her or Leslie in her relationship with Christine. Brigid squeezed Ryan's arm in reply and they walked together toward the dining room.

Christine's youthful wonder and wide-eyed admiration afforded those more accustomed to McKinley an opportunity to see the dining room as though for the first time. The young woman seemed to take in the sight of the wood floors and walls, gilded ceiling, fireplace and Waterford chandelier like she had walked into a long-harbored dream. "It's grand! You're so lucky to live like this," she expressed with yearning.

Leslie encouraged Christine to sit at the lavish table making no attempt to hide her glowing pleasure in having her home appreciated. "Come back later this weekend if you can get free. I'll be happy to show you around inside . . . and outside if the weather stays nice."

"Would you?" Christine asked excitedly. "I'd like that very much."

"Any time, just call ahead." Leslie was feeling more kinship with this young lady as the evening progressed.

Well into the third course Ryan introduced the subject of her beloved project: the art institute for women. She explained the concept to Brigid and Christine and received an enthusiastic response from both of them.

"Your father would have been proud of you, Ryan. The art

world needs all the people with vision it can muster. Is there any way I can help?" Brigid asked hopefully.

"In fact there is. It would make me happy if you would consider the position of co-administrator of the program. It would take some time away from your own art, but I believe the rewards would make up for that loss," Ryan suggested.

Brigid was surprised and pleased by being asked to serve in the capacity that was more than token. But *co*-administrator. She had to know what that meant. "With whom?"

Ryan provided the answer casually. "Leslie."

Brigid's eyes enlarged noticeably as did Christine's. This was the best proof yet that Brigid had been taken back into the trusted status she had once enjoyed. "Honestly?" Brigid had to ask, wondering if she were dreaming.

"Truly, Brig," Leslie confirmed. She touched the redhead's hand lightly. "Say you'll take the job. We need you."

A nod from Ryan and a squeeze from Christine, and Brigid was convinced. "Well, absolutely. It would be my pleasure." Her face beamed with joy.

"Excellent," Ryan said as she raised her glass in toast. "To the Serle Art Institute for Women."

"Hear, hear," Leslie, Brigid and Christine assented in unison as their glasses touched in harmony.

Pink, mauve, scarlet, coral, and cream were the dominant colors in the dazzling scheme that decorated the morning sky as the brilliant rolling carpet unfurled in advance of the fireball chariot, the sun. Birds paid tribute and the winds bowed in silence—it was a sunrise to remember, to paste into the mind's album of perfect moments in life.

Leslie and Ryan hadn't spoken since its beginning. Their coffee was tepid and their breakfast cakes untouched. Their hands had sought each other's over the glass table in the solarium where they took their first meal of the day. These lovers were one, joined in spirit and heart, taking in this display as though it were created for them alone. (It was.)

When the show faded into a wistful, pale blend of pinks they shared a knowing look and turned their attention to what each had meant to do before the matchless beauty performed for them: Leslie to her morning paper, Ryan to her calculator and flight plan.

A servant lingering nearby took the resumption of activity as her cue to replace the coffee cups with new, filled ones. The morning had begun, perfectly.

"I want to go south today," Ryan stated. "There's a high pressure system over the Sangre de Christos and the clouds are due to burn off which would give us a clear view by the time we got there."

Leslie envisioned the rugged mountain range with all its sharp contrasts and grinned—that kind of remote beauty was just what she craved just then. "Mmm, that would be nice. Maybe land on a frozen lake somewhere and . . . " she let her seductive pause open her lover's imagination for making the best of moments of solitude promised by inaccessible lakes above ten thousand feet during what was still the height of winter in the Rocky Mountains.

Ryan chuckled gruffly and reached over to twist Leslie's nipple through her satin robe. "And . . . we'll take the Harley to the airport," she advised her wife with mock threat in her voice.

"Ohhh, oonn, Ryan," Leslie moaned. "Yes, let's," she responded sexily, thinking ahead to the thrill of being Ryan's passenger on the massive, powerful motorcycle. It was a melting thought; breakfast wouldn't be finished a moment too soon.

Watching Ryan kick start her motorcycle was a never-ending source of amazement for Leslie. To see this slender, seemingly weightless figure of a woman exert such strength with such ease was nothing short of thrilling for her. Taking her place behind Ryan opened up the doors of her senses making it possible for her to experience each exhilerating sensation this mode of transportation had to offer.

Ryan belonged on this rugged machine the same way she belonged in the left seat of an airplane or grasping a woman in passion—it was part of who she was. For all that, the neighbors had yet to grow accustomed to seeing this wealthy woman storm out the gates of McKinley on her fire-breathing chopper. Even less easy for them to grasp was the sight of the refined and gracious woman of the house behind Ryan on the Harley. If encountered, these neighbors stared or raised their noses, and Leslie giggled every time. She knew that, more than anything, it was the display of raw sexual power that bothered them. It bothered her, too, right between her legs. She was dampening her chamois slacks even before they got to the first stop light.

The rhythmic throbbing beneath her body; Ryan's flowing, commanding body in front of her, the biting wind all around her, the glorious thunder of harnessed might resounding through her; in the face of it all, Leslie could barely contain her excitement. Ryan leaned in and out of the freeway traffic, almost oblivious to the intensity of the moment. But she was keenly aware of it all; she could look casual and untouched because that was how she went through life: on the edge. There was no other place to live life from as far as she was concerned and she had always been there.

Ryan wanted her lover settled down before they reached the airport; she reached a hand behind her and pressed her gloved fingers into the moist place between her wife's legs. Seconds later Leslie's fingers were digging into Ryan's upper arms with a force that could be felt through the thick leather of her bomber jacket. Shortly after that the passenger's hands grabbed Ryan's fingers painfully and flattened them against the now convulsing sex she had just administered to. Leslie was not quiet about her orgasm — quite the contrary — it was fortunate they were speeding along a noisy freeway else she be thought in dire pain, rather than in utter satisfaction.

By the time they reached the airport Leslie was exhibiting the half-lidded contentment of a well cared for lover. She followed about airily as Ryan filed her flight plan and prepared the single engine, four-seater Cessna for their journey to the mountains. Phil Peterson came out of his office to assist and was greeted by Ryan.

"Hi, Phil," Ryan welcomed her mentor warmly.

"Hey, Ryan. Sorry I couldn't get out here sooner, got hung up on the phone. How are you?" Phil asked paternally. It was a manner of speaking that he used more and more as he neared the end of his fifth decade. Practically half his life had been spent loving and caring about Ryan.

Ryan just smiled in reply. Phil knew her like a book and never really had to ask how she was. What Phil really wanted was to be near Leslie. He immediately ducked under the plane to help her into the right side of it, solicitously fastening her seat belt and checking on her comfort like an adoring puppy eager to please at any cost. Leslie let him fuss for a moment, then thanked him, her cue to Ryan to rescue her from his pampering attentions.

"Phil? Is this log book up to date?" Ryan asked absently; she knew it was.

Phil's rugged complexion did little to hide his blush when he realized he was making a fool of himself over Ryan's wife again. He had never learned any other way to show gratitude to Leslie for helping Ryan turn her life around and find happiness. Abruptly he excused himself and walked around to the other side of the airplane.

"Sure is, buddy," he answered confidently. He ran a tight ship at his flight service, and no one knew it better than Ryan.

"Come here for a minute," Ryan requested as she put her arm around the back of Phil's leathery neck and led him a few feet away from the plane. "I was thinking about something last night. I take you completely for granted. I've always just assumed that you would be there for me no matter what I did. But I've never thanked you for it."

"You don't have to, Ryan. My thanks come from being able to be with you and help you. Ever since that first day you came to me and stated in a vaguely Irish accent that you were going to learn to fly I've known you were the student and comrade I've always wanted to share my love of flying with. My logical mind told me that you were a brilliant, intense seven year old girl (even if your father insisted you were a boy, I knew better), and that you were being arrogant and unrealistic. When I looked into those stubborn jade eyes of yours, I knew none of that mattered. You were going to do whatever you set your mind to, and I'm damn glad I didn't laugh in your face. You're a comfort to me, Ryan, always have been." Phil's pale blue eyes were soft with love and devotion.

Ryan took her mirrored sunglasses off slowly and returned his look. Without warning, for the first time in her life, Ryan kissed Phil on the cheek and spoke from her heart words she had not said the twenty-six years she'd known him. "I love you, Phil."

Phil was a sensitive man, and never let the artificial standards of manhood stand in the way where love was concerned. He patted Ryan's side affectionately and nodded. "I've loved you more than my own children, a fact they have never cared for, but you are what has made my life worth living." He could tell he was going to cry soon and didn't want to; it was no way to send a friend off on a recreational flight. "Hey, you kids have a good trip today. You always seem to pick the good ones, don't you?" Phil asked, referring to the excellent weather.

Ryan gave her friend a squeeze on the arm and put her glasses back on. "Yes, sir, I do," she called jokingly to him as she pulled the blocks from the front tire then boarded the plane.

Phil waved to them and watched until they rounded a building, taxiing out of sight toward the runway for take-off.

Leslie seldom spoke when she was in a plane with Ryan. Her joy was derived from watching her beloved in her element. Having no interest in learning to fly herself, Leslie was content to savor these quiet times, marveling at the graceful way Ryan handled herself in the sky. Each hand movement on the controls fascinated Leslie. Normally bursting with curiosity and questions, she sensed Ryan felt no need to teach or be interrupted by the idle inquiries. Instead Leslie let the entire process remain shrouded in mystery, a thing to cause wonder and enchantment. She looked on as Ryan worked the pedals at her feet (Phil had once said that Ryan had the lightest touch he'd ever encountered) and listened to the occasional chatter going back and forth between various towers or other pilots who came into view.

Ryan's eyesight was as close as a human's could come to being eagle-like; she never missed anything in the sky or on the ground. Her keen alertness and lightning reflexes kept the mood around her lively but somehow peaceful. Unlike many other things a person could do with Ryan, flying with her was always the only truly safe one. Once in the sky there was no challenge she was not equal to; she was untouched by the world and its troubles, master of her universe.

Leslie could relax when she was Ryan's passenger in the sky. Here was the one place where no one would interfere with their love or happiness; this was free time, protected from harm. Sanctuary. Before she realized it they were already above the mountains with their brilliant snow-covered expanses.

They took their time: Ryan pointing out the wildlife when she spotted it, including a magnificent herd of elk sauntering along in search of food. They climbed higher, it got colder. Leslie was glad she'd worn badger; Ryan seemed untouched by the chill. From time to time Leslie would feel a warm flush and she would know Ryan was staring at her. In all their time together Ryan had still not grown completely accustomed to Leslie's striking beauty—it was level with anything Nature had to offer below.

When Ryan navigated over the crest of an upright jagged mountain a spectacular lake situated in a bowl came into view. Everything about the site was crisp, primordial and irresistibly inviting. Upon closer inspection the lovers were certain that they had found the inaccessible, forbidding lake they had been looking for. It was the sort of place one would expect to find some missing-link cousins to homo sapiens roaming about. It was *that* remote.

Ryan was at her best in finding a way to land her plane on the surface of the frozen lake. It might be a challenge to get back out again, but Ryan loved challenges. Thinking about being alone with Leslie in this forgotten place made Ryan wonder if she cared if they ever did get out again. But land she did, and upon bringing the plane to a full stop she saw instantly that there would be a clear path out again.

Leslie was glowing with pride. "Excellently well done," she praised. Her face was aglow, shimmering ethereally as if she had been introduced to some deity of high places and virgin spaces in time.

"Thank you, madam. I do believe this place bears exploring. Wouldn't you agree?" Ryan invited as she settled the plane and opened her door, grabbing a blanket and binoculars.

"Without delay," Leslie assented, stopping only to pick up the thermos of lentil soup and package of goat cheese with flat bread. They struck out over the untouched layer of fresh snow toward the near wall bathed in sun. Somehow, they knew they would discover a sheltered, warm shelf to dine on and look about from. Ryan cleared away the powdered snow and spread the blanket. Leslie took the utensils from her pocket and they indulged in a hearty mountain meal.

Finishing first, Ryan took the binoculars and began to scan the walls around them. She showed her lover the trio of mountain goats looking down at them from a precarious ledge, then two hares, all enjoyed thoroughly by Leslie. Ryan took the glasses back to get a better look at something she thought she saw a few hundred feet away and resting still.

"Leslie," Ryan whispered without fear. "Just to the left of the shadow, up on the second ledge . . . I think it's a female." Ryan handed the binoculars back to her lover.

Leslie found the animal easily. "Ryan," she breathed, "she's wonderful! Look how alert, yet casual she is." No sooner than each of them had seen her, the great mountain lioness disappeared into a cave in the shadows. It was a thrilling sight.

When Leslie turned to her mate, Ryan had that look in her eye, the look that was equally thrilling and never failed to stir Leslie. It was a look that said, "I *want* you, and I will *have* you. *Now*."

And far be it from Leslie to disagree. She did what she always did: her breathing deepened, she became softer, enticing, ready. Ryan was the sort of woman you simply did not deny. If she wanted you, she got you. That in itself was exciting, but knowing what Ryan could do to you when she did get you was enough to make even the most devout ascetic stir under her robes. And Leslie was *not* an ascetic.

"Ryan," Leslie panted. Her senses were sharpened to a heightened pitch nearly beyond her ability to manage. What she needed more than anything else was to be released from the strain—and no one was more qualified than Ryan to do just that.

"Leslie," Ryan replied darkly. Her need to defuse the buildup was just as great.

"Ryan." Leslie eased herself onto her back and took off her sunglasses so her lover could *see* the need. Her eyes were begging. "Ryan," she whispered desperately.

"What, baby?"

"Ohh,"

"What do you want, lover?" Ryan baited.

"You," Leslie cooed.

"Is that all?" Ryan teased meanly. "You've got me, I'm right here." She leaned over her lover, bringing her face to a fraction of an inch out of kissing range.

"I want you," Leslie restated frantically.

"Want me? For what?"

"Oh, Ryan." Leslie tried unsuccessfully to be kissed. "I want you to take me," she spoke softly—her conviction undermined by her need.

"Pardon me?" Ryan said sarcastically. "I don't believe I heard you."

Leslie could bear it no longer. "Take me!" she wailed, pulling her sex partner atop her soft and well-furred body.

Ryan was undone by her wife's need. "Gooooddd,' she moaned. Their lips mashed together and Ryan forced Leslie's legs apart to mount her. Blind, animalistic, divine madness overtook them and they took each other to the other side of need where fulfillment is a gift of love, a combining of souls. Their bodies heaved and thrust into one another's until their screams of lust and joy became indistinguishable from the shrill cry of the falcon that called out the celebration of life above them.

It was the shadow turning its chilling blanket over them that brought them back to the reality that they did have to return. One last look about the mountain paradise and the couple boarded the plane. Ryan took their bodies out of the dark cavern, but for all time a piece of their hearts and souls would remain in that frost-laden, forbidden world of winter. They bade it farewell with one last flyover and a secret smile, then headed north again, happy, as one.

10

Ryan's eyes came open suddenly. It was three o'clock in the morning; in the still darkness there was no difficulty in sensing something had changed. As if by instinct she leaned over to turn on her bedside lamp. During the brief moment while her eyes grew accustomed to the light, Ryan wished the time hadn't come so soon. She didn't want to turn over to look at Leslie, but she knew she must.

The perpetual peace that reigned over Leslie's countenance was as enduring as ever, and brought a loving smile to Ryan's face as she recalled the many times she had stayed awake just to watch her lover sleep. But there was something more profound and beautiful about her appearance than usual. Ryan was awed by the perfection, the exquisiteness of this resting woman. For long minutes she looked on as tears came to her eyes clouding her vision; it was almost more than she could bear. She reached out to touch the smooth skin and found it was still warm to the touch. Leslie's presence was nearby.

Enlisting her courage, Ryan forced herself into a healer's state to search inside Leslie's body for the cause of death: a stroke. She had gone quickly and painlessly; Ryan was grateful. With a deep, struggling inhale Ryan composed herself so her soul could speak to that of her beloved. "It is time then?" she asked resignedly.

Leslie's spirit self, Venadia, answered encouragingly, "Yes, my love." The angelic sweetness of the voice she heard in her mind relaxed Ryan.

"Very well then. I shall be along shortly." Ryan's voice now sounded filled with purpose and bravery.

"I await you," Venadia reassured calmly.

Ryan arose from the bed of love to take a quick shower and dry her hair. Her body prepared, she ceremoniously dressed in a black silk day suit and tie with a white shirt. She tied the laces of her black shoes and went to Leslie's closets where she found the gold lace gown Leslie loved best along with the cream and gold heels that matched the dress. Together with the delicate under-things she chose, Ryan laid the clothes out and straightened the bed. When she was satisfied that all was well she turned to seek out Sanji and Corelle.

In the stark, white slave quarters, Sanji slept like a child without a care. Ryan awakened her gently. "Sanji, I need you."

Sanji stirred softly, her eyes opened abruptly and she looked oddly at Ryan's attire. She sensed something was amiss, but unquestioningly replied, "As you wish, Master."

"Put your robe on and come with me," Ryan instructed her.

Sanji did as she was told and followed Ryan into Corelle's room. She stood patiently next to the large brass bed watching as Ryan roused the servant.

"Corelle, I need you."

Corelle floated out of her restful sleep and gazed wide-eyed at her Master. "I am yours, Master," answered the young woman, who Leslie had cherished so. Her room was lighted solely by the beam of light coming from the hallway; she could only just make out that Ryan was dressed differently than she normally would in the wee hours of the morning. Sanji's presence did nothing to tell her what was needed of her.

"Put your robe on," Ryan told her firmly.

Corelle obeyed quietly then awaited her next instructions.

Ryan spoke seriously to the two faithful bondswomen. "Sanji, Corelle. I wish you to come with me, but I must have your promise that when you see what I am about to show you that you will not cry out and awaken the household. Do I have your promise?"

Sanji and Corelle shared a puzzled look but agreed and followed their Master down the hall to the nuptial bedroom. Ryan put her arm around each of her charges and guided them toward the bed.

Sanji was the first to respond. She had looked upon the face of death many times in her native Jamaica. Her knees went out from under her and she fell on them to the floor. She groaned loudly but did not cry out. "Ohh, no." Never before had she felt love, true love, for her Mistress, but the years of animosity fled in that sharp moment. "My sweet Mistress," she whispered into her hands which she had brought to her mouth to keep herself quiet.

Corelle was bewildered by Sanji's behavior. She let her eyes feast upon her Mistress and thought to herself how quiet and lovely she appeared. So still. Suddenly fear and disbelief settled into her heart. Her voice quivered. "Master, what is wrong?"

Ryan could tell from the panic in the young woman's voice that she would not be able to keep her promise. She placed her hand over Corelle's mouth as she informed her gently and with extreme compassion, "Corelle, your Mistress is dead."

Corelle's eyes opened wider than wide, her breathing quickened, building to a pitch in preparation for a heart-wrenching wail. Ryan's hand tightened about her mouth to muffle it. When the girl slackened in her grip she let go knowing that Corelle had come back to a sense of her self and purpose in life. Corelle remembered that she promised not to cry out and caught her breath.

"Corelle, I need you to control yourself. I need your help here." Ryan's voice was firm with the command that worked best with the servant which produced instant results.

At once, Corelle's thoughts turned to her Mistress. Her face relaxed and the calm composure that accompanied bonded service displayed itself where once had been searing, blinding pain. Ryan let go of her mouth and stroked her hair. "Thank you."

She turned to look down at Sanji who was wrapped around her leg but no longer weeping. Sanji spoke frantically, "Master, please don't leave me. Please." She sounded almost childlike in her plaintiveness.

Ryan leaned over to speak to her. With her hand she grasped the quivering chin and held the face up. "Sanji, don't be absurd. I can't go on without her. I must *go*."

"I can't bear to live without you, Master," the desperate slave pleaded.

"Come with us then." Ryan's invitation was calm and sincere.

Sanji's face transformed instantly. The thought had never occurred to her. It was, of course, the only reasonable action for her to take. She answered without hesitation. "Will you have me?"

"We will be honored." Ryan had known for some time that Sanji would follow her beyond this existence. She wasn't as sure about Corelle.

Corelle watched this exchange carefully. In her time with Ryan's slave, she had learned a great deal about devotion from Sanji. She was normally quite innocent about things such as her Master and Sanji were discussing, but in the face of death her mind was clear and rational.

Ryan gazed into Sanji's large eyes a moment longer, savoring the awesome devotion she saw in them. Then she turned to Corelle.

"Corelle, you need not follow if you wish otherwise. I have provided quite handsomely for you in my will. You could grow up and be an independent woman of means, or stay here and serve Brigid. The choice is yours," Ryan offered carefully, not wanting to sway the girl with the passion of the moment.

Corelle looked at Ryan and then to her Mistress. "Master," she inquired, "is she as beautiful in the spirit world?"

Ryan looked lovingly at her wife and replied honestly, "Only the Great Goddess herself is more so."

Corelle sighed happily, imagining it. "How will you find her?"

"She is here about. Waiting," Ryan revealed.

Corelle looked up suddenly as though she could see Leslie. She spoke with a solemn maturity. "I love you, Milady — to the ends of the Earth and beyond. I wish to be by your side."

To Ryan: "Master, I do not wish to be left behind to mourn your deaths. Please take me with you."

Ryan knew Corelle's mind was made up, and that she had no regrets or misgivings. "You are welcome to join us, Corelle. I shall." She brought Sanji to her feet and addressed them both. "I want you to bathe yourselves and dress in what she would like best on you. Then come back here and cleanse her; put her clothes on. I have some letters to write. I will be back shortly. Go about this last service to your Mistress quietly and reverently." They both agreed solemnly and left to follow her instructions.

Ryan went to her study and opened the safe. From it she took the diamond necklace and ring she wished Leslie to wear one last time, a small vial, and two packets of papers. She sat at her desk and began to write.

Dearest friend and cousin, Brigid,

My beloved Leslie died in the night of a stroke. She went as peacefully and courageously into death as she ever did into life. You, better than anyone, know that I cannot go on without her. Our slaves, Sanji and Corelle, chose, willingly, to join us on our journey to the spirit world beyond. It is not your destiny to follow us or I would have asked you to come as well.

It may seem unfair to you that my stay here with Leslie was cut short in its prime. Take heart. Fleeting though it was — our moment together was both glorious and beautiful. Please, when you remember us, do so with love, faith and hope.

Leslie has, forever and always, been my one true love. We have been so since the beginning of time. If we prevail in this final struggle we will become one for all eternity. There is but one who can tear us asunder. Lest this letter fall into the wrong hands, I dare not mention the name of the soul, but you know of whom I speak.

You, Brigid, have taught me the true meaning of friendship. I thank you for that. Even in our darkest hour, we were able to find our deepest selves and preserve our faithful friendship. Absolving you, and Rags, has been difficult for me, but in so doing I've received a gift: during my sojourn in this lifetime I have learned forgiveness. The value of this lesson is something I cannot begin to express in the limited terms of this clumsy language.

I realize that my actions will visit great grief upon you. I will do what I can to lessen it at every turn. By way of consolation, I will tell you that you have met your true great love in this lifetime. Christine will love you more than anyone ever has, and you will find, soon, that you love her more than any other. She will serve you and be your helpmate for the rest of your long, happy life.

Bonnie will serve you for the rest of her days also. Be warned: they are numbered. Her grief will consume her and you must witness yet one more life expire, a product of the O'Donnell legacy of sorrow.

I have left you specific instructions for the handling of our bodies, along with copies of our wills (Barbara McFarland is the executrix), and the plans for the Serle Art Institute for

Women. Since Leslie will not be here to share the position of administrator, please accept the position of director along with the substantial salary I have arranged for you. I know you don't need the money, but the details have been arranged so that you can avoid paying inheritance taxes that might cause you to lose McKinley. It would please Leslie and me if you and Christine would live in McKinley, and love it the way we have and would if we had stayed.

For now, my friend, I must say good-bye for us all. When your time comes to reach over, you will know if Leslie and I have succeeded — we will be there to greet you.

All my love,

Ryan O'Donnell

My dearest Bonnie,

Throughout my life, from beginning to end, you have served me with the purest devotion. I am deeply grateful to you. Your final reward will be pleasant and peaceful, as you have always wished it would be.

Your life has been but one long vigil. You have watched and watched, with heavy heart — first as my sweet mother sacrificed her life so that I might live, then my father as he died daily for twenty-five years that I might grow. I know you loved him sweetly and kindly. I also know you saw me the day I began to die inside, and you watched.

The debt you are paying is almost paid. In the end you will be free. It is my wish that you serve Brigid in my stead. She is soon to wed Miss Latham, and one day be happy and fulfilled. There are numerous paintings of Brigid's behind a panel in the wine cellar, ones she created during her madness when she lived with us. Once Brigid is recovered from the worst part of her grief, please see that her art is taken out of hiding and returned to her. She will not destroy them.

My only explanation for what has happened this day is that it

is part of a grand design. If the outcome is what I wish it to be, I shall, along with my beloved, greet you on your passing.
Your faithful friend,

Ryan O'Donnell

Dearest Christine,
I wish you to know always of my very great love for you. I am glad you will be able to comfort Brigid in her hour of need.
Thank you,

Ryan O'Donnell

These letters Ryan sealed in envelopes and wrote the appropriate names on them. She wrote one more which was to remain an open letter to the authorities.
To whom it may concern,
You doubtless wish to know what has happened here. I beg of you to respect my wishes and refrain from performing autopsies on our bodies. I shall tell you all you wish to know.
Miss Leslie Anne Serle passed on this morning of natural causes: a stroke. My skills as a healer and diagnostician have been documented completely. This information is available from my attorney, Barbara McFarland. Use that information to satisfy yourselves that what I tell you is true.
I, Ryan O'Donnell, of County Donegal, Ireland, have purposely and willingly consumed a fatal dose of a fast-acting poison derived from toxic plant material, which you may feel free to analyze. I have done so that I may join my beloved wife in the non-physical world.
Miss Sanji Charles of Jamaica begged for and was granted the privilege of joining Miss Serle and myself. She, too, will-

ingly accepted a lethal dose of this same poison which she administered to herself.

Miss Corelle Trant of County Kerry, Ireland, did request passage to the other side as well. She, of her own will, decided that she did not wish to be left behind to mourn the deaths of her Mistress, Master, and fellow servant. To this end, she willingly consumed the above-mentioned poison.

The manner in which we have taken our lives may seem ritualistic and crazed to you. This is of no concern to us. We began as we wish to go on. I ask that the press behave honorably toward those who have been left behind.

Respectfully,

Ryan O'Donnell

Ryan put her pen down and picked up the small bottle. She held it in her hand for a moment, staring at the ancient runes carved in the seal. Sighing resolutely, she gathered the jewels, packets and letters and left her den for the last time.

In the master suite, her instructions had been carried out precisely and quickly. Leslie's body was dressed splendidly; Corelle had fixed her hair in a graceful sweep and applied makeup expertly. Sanji had slipped some white violets from the greenhouse into Leslie's hair. Leslie's body was lying in gentle repose; the effect was radiant.

The slaves were dressed in the colors assigned to them: Sanji in blue and silver, Corelle in ivory and jade. Their faces were clear and patient.

Ryan brought two chairs to the foot of the bed and motioned to them to sit. She left the packets and letters where they would be found easily, put the jewelry on her wife's body, and took three small glasses from the decanter set on the dresser. Into these she poured the proper dosage of the poison and handed one to each of her slaves. Sanji and Corelle took their glasses reverently, as though they were being given a precious gift.

Fully clothed and lying next to her sweet lover, Ryan reassured her slaves. "This will not hurt, nor will it last more than a minute. Your heart will simply stop."

Before taking part in the fatal ritual she held her glass up in toast. "Leslie, my love, we follow you to death and beyond." They drank of the liquid and dropped their glasses. Ryan stretched out on the bed and gathered Leslie's body in her arms for one last kiss.

The last thing Corelle saw on this Earth was her Master loving her Mistress.

The last thing Sanji saw on this Earth was her Master loving her Mistress.

The last thing Ryan saw on this Earth was her beloved's peaceful face.

11

Venadia watched the early morning preparations for death with some small sense of regret. It had been necessary to end her life in her sleep to keep Ryan from interfering. The time had come for the battle to begin and there was no turning back. Her stay in the physical world was to be Venadia's last. No matter what the outcome of the ensuing struggle, she could not go back, could not experience the bittersweet poignancy of the joy and pain that only the physical world could offer. There were no more lessons to be learned from her beloved planet; she must reside in the spirit world for all time — if she survived.

Regret turned to knowing contentment when she witnessed both her handmaidens agreeing, without hesitation, to join her in the other world. There had never been any doubt in her mind that they would wish to be with her, wherever she was.

All was going smoothly . . . the waiting was over . . . in an instant it was done. Venadia rose from her bench to greet those she loved above all others.

Blaise became her whole, spirit-self before Venadia: thick grey robes hooded and mantled the womanly form, obscuring her dynamic strength. Clustered about her lovely oval face were masses of charcoal-colored hair. But it was her fervid red eyes that held the beholder, drawing attention away from the burning necklace of power about her neck or the pyrope ring on her finger or the black-diamond scalloping on her hemline. This was a visage of controlled, yet excitable power — untried power, indeterminate ability, unpredictable will.

"Welcome, my love." Venadia opened her Veiled arms happily. The heartbreak that had once separated them was healed and forgotten. Their oneness had overcome adversity.

Because they were not alone, Blaise did not raise the gauzy fabric that shrouded Venadia's ivory, porcelain beauty but allowed herself to be taken into the delicate embrace of the fascinating Queen. Eyes closed and silent, they let their love pass between them for a nourishing, albeit brief, moment. Destiny was breathing down their necks.

Blaise stepped aside to allow the two handmaidens who had followed her to come forward to show reverence to their Queen. In unison the two maids, now in their true states, knelt at Venadia's feet and kissed the hem of her Veils.

Venadia spoke the ancient names she had given them as she recognized and brought each of them to their feet to be welcomed. The maid who had been Sanji in the physical world rose first to the sound of her name, the one she had used in a previous life: Lizack.

"Lizack, your place at my side has not been filled by another. It is still my wish that you serve me. I bid you to return," Venadia ordered kindly.

The youth who gave the appearance of having been carved from ebony stepped to the left of Venadia, bowing and smiling elatedly. "Nothing pleases me more than to serve you, My Queen. I am grateful that you still find me acceptable as your handmaiden." Lizack spoke quickly in a small voice chosen carefully to show her humbleness and to avoid taxing her Queen with effusive gratefulness. Nothing more needed to be said between them. To be allowed to continue her loyal service was all Lizack required from her existence.

Venadia addressed her second handmaiden, Coré, who had been Corelle in the physical world, just as she had spoken to Lizack. Looking for all like a figurine sculpted of white marble, Coré took her place on Venadia's right, shyly uttering her thanks. "I shall serve you always, My Queen, in any way you require." Fulfilled and entranced by her Queen's beauty, Coré was a model of true happiness and peace.

Suddenly agitated, Venadia refrained from showing her maids the deep affection and appreciation she felt for them.

The call was upon her; the time was at hand. Gathering her Veils in her hand to give her room to walk briskly, she breezed by her mate toward a heavy drape that hung over the entrance to a long hallway. "Come, we must go quickly now. The Council will not be kept waiting any longer." She held aside the drape to show the way; she had waited until the last possible moment, extending the time of loving to its inevitable end.

The three went ahead of their Queen, according to custom. At the end of the hall they stood briefly at the fork; Venadia and Blaise gazing at one another for a last adoring look before Blaise was required to walk the round hall to the formal entrance to the Council chambers.

"Strength be with you, my darling," Venadia whispered to her mate as they separated. She then swept gracefully behind her maids, signaling to the court youth in the antechamber to have her arrival announced. She didn't listen to any of the protracted proclamation, and Lizack had to tug gently on her Veil to shake her from her sad reverie. Venadia had been announced, there was nowhere to go except to her Throne—this one last time. She wasn't surprised that she felt relieved the process had begun, the waiting over.

Blaise paced about aimlessly in the waiting room outside the Council chambers. She had remained silent in an effort to calm herself and still her raging thoughts. Unlike her mate, Blaise couldn't make a casual transition through death to the spirit world. Each time, the transformation was accomplished with an inner violence that dissipated her energies and made it nearly impossible to function well at all. Uppermost in her mind was not the demon demi-goddess in the next room, but her loved ones back on the physical plane who would be discovering the bodies she and the others had left behind, the waste. Blaise couldn't shake the compassion and she needed to; it was critical if she were to concentrate on what she must do.

While there had been advantages to her brief stay on Earth, Blaise knew Anara had the upper hand for having stayed in the spirit world, honing her skills, lobbying for support among those who could assist her in the upcoming battle. Blaise did not feel prepared, and even less so when a courtier opened the door to her small cell to request her presence in the main Council chambers. She had no doubt that the instant she walked into that large, ancient room everyone there would sense her turmoil. She nodded to the attendant to lead the way. Allowing her hood to fall around her face to hide her eyes, she tried to center herself as she followed him. Focusing on the fiery necklace on her chest, she spoke her name inside her own mind, building power to defend herself from the onslaught of negative energy she was sure to encounter upon setting foot on the round symbol in the middle of the great chamber.

She ignored Anara entirely as they walked, side by side, to the brilliant red, green and gold triangles set in a circle of royal blue. This was a place of power and illusion. Controlled by a passive, benign force, such as Venadia's, the circle could be harnessed and used for great good (and had been for eons under the peaceful Queen's guidance). If left to the likes of Anara, Blaise reminded herself, the symbol could summon tragedy and destruction, herald the loss of freedom for entire races — a dangerous tool.

That sobering thought was closely followed by a pain near Blaise's left temple. Involuntarily, her hand came up to massage it. Unbeknownst to her, that show of weakness cost her the support of one of the council members: Bilouge. *Her* only concern was to stop listening to the wail of sorrow that collectively arose from those she had left behind.

Then she heard two things simultaneously. Firmly and soundly Venadia's voice penetrated her thoughts with an abrupt admonition only she could here. "Let them *go*, Blaise!" But it was the snide chuckle that came from the malicious woman standing next to her that shook Blaise from her linkage with the physical world. She summoned her strength, broke away from the past and stood erect to face the Council.

Carefully, Blaise scanned its members and noted the presence of four who were not members: Venadia's handmaidens, Lizack and Coré, Anara's handmaiden, Fila, and, measuring her own wary hesitation, Blaise looked in the direction of Hestia, the Goddess of Fire. Hestia had already been instrumental in assuring that this battle would go on as planned by recovering the necklace which held Blaise's power within it and giving it to her.

It was no secret that the Goddess of Fire had more than a cursory interest in the outcome of this battle. Hestia could not abide Anara and would chafe under her influence should the white-eyed opponent win The Throne. But Blaise wondered if the flame-like image of Hestia would mind so much if she, Blaise, were out of the way, leaving the path to Venadia's heart clear. It was an unsettling prospect and Blaise did not linger on it. Instead she let her eyes rest upon her lover and mate, being in no hurry to see how her opponent was dressed, which she knew would be pleasing if not outright unchaste.

"Lewd is more like it," Venadia broadcasted to her lover via their private thought wavelength. The Queen looked over the low-cut velvet and ermine dress Anara had woven about her body and wondered why she didn't just wear the jewels alone (which were plentiful) for she couldn't have been any more revealing. Long, scalloped panels of velvet were suspended from a fur waistband forming a skirt which called attention to Anara's long legs and well-shaped hips and backside.

Her entrance had been as distracting as it was grand: each step she had taken had given someone a view of something. Including Venadia, whom Anara had yet to look at. There was something disarming about showing an enemy one's sex in an almost blatant manner. The effect was not lost on Venadia, although it was scarcely the one Anara had hoped to produce. Anara was unaware that instead of the anger she had planned for, she'd forced the Queen to stifle uncharacteristically bold laughter.

Venadia wished she could be as lighthearted about the results of her mental survey of the Council members. They were seated in a half circle in various poses of preeminence — earlier they had been huddled in clusters, lobbying for support to the last. This was to be expected, but the Queen had watched closely all the same.

She had paid particular attention to the one fully male member, Ramonye. It was well known he fancied himself irresistible, and next in line for a place on The Throne — as Anara's consort. This didn't trouble Venadia. What gave her pause was watching the elegant man paying attention to the hermaphrodite, Bilouge. Blaise was in need of all the energy she could muster to back up her bid for the seat of power. Bilouge was one of the three members who might make their energy available in the fight to come. If Bilouge could be swayed to Anara's side, for whatever reason, there would remain but the females who had jurisdiction over creativity and life — Serdon and Pliquay respectively — to back Blaise. And, of course, Venadia herself.

Now that the battle was about to commence it was obvious the larger measure of advantage had fallen to Anara. With Ramonye, and now Bilouge, the Goddess of Light, and the warrioress Caspia, all ready to bolster Anara's power should she request their aid, Blaise's future was uncertain at best.

And Anara knew it. The vixenish contender moved her eyes from one end of those seated before her with challenging pride to the other—dipping her gaze uncertainly in the middle of the semi-circle where The Throne she so coveted was situated. When she had first entered the Chamber, the sight of the soon-to-be-dethroned-Queen filled the corner of her eye. Anara had caught glimpses of the Veiled Queen in times past, but had never looked directly at her. She was both relieved and annoyed that Venadia was still Veiled. However difficult it was to look at the Queen, it was easier when she was Veiled. But a part of Anara wanted Venadia exposed, like everyone else.

What are you waiting for? Anara chastised herself. Puffing up with self-importance, Anara found herself to raise her eyes to take in the sight of the ivory Veils draped over the hidden form with the splendor of water frozen in free fall. Somehow, Anara wasn't prepared to be unable to see the Queen's face. Without warning, Anara found herself jealous of the unseen beauty. She knew a modicum of envy—wishing she had acquired that anonymous, self-containment for herself.

Anara recalled how the Goddess of Light had warned her that the Queen was not easily shaken, given to few words, and dangerous in her shroud of silence. Anara could see now that her friend and ally had not exaggerated. Becoming aware that the others on the Council were watching for her reaction to their ruler, Anara masked her misgivings neatly and smiled nonchalantly. First impressions were everything here and she couldn't risk losing any of the support she'd worked for. Certainly Blaise hadn't fared well among those gathered in the ancient place but Anara had to reinforce her confident posture. She did so be being the first to turn to face her opponent.

While waiting for Blaise to do the same, a new thought occurred to Anara. Never before had the reigning Queen Regent been the lover of one of the contenders for that title. What forces might come into play because of that situation were unknown to Anara. And she didn't like not knowing all the variables—especially ones that involved that most unpredictable of emotions: love. She made a mental note to request the special assistance of the Goddess of Light in this matter.

With the grim determination that had characterized her entire attitude toward her position as a contender for The Throne,

Blaise turned to look at her opponent. Her face was still hidden from most of those seated in Council; they did not see her close her eyes against the sight of Anara's splendor. Blaise could neither forget her desire for the seductress nor her hatred of Anara's treachery. Her conflicting feelings were scored upon her heart like brands, and played upon her face distressfully as though she were wincing from the blows of a whip.

While none were better situated to see under the hood than Anara, it was the Goddess of Light who had the proper line of sight and motive to watch, and watch carefully. She knew Anara wouldn't pay close enough attention to the subtle signals Blaise gave away; Anara was entirely too sure of herself to notice. But it was this greedy Goddess, and her polar opposite, Venadia (sensing her lover's dilemma), who took note of Blaise's vulnerability.

The Goddess of Light began to plan how to take advantage of this weakness. Venadia took pity on her mate, saddened by the knowledge that Blaise had to learn for herself the way to solve her internal struggle; that she could be of no assistance to her lover. This would, in all likelihood be a fight to death. The lines had been drawn. The time was now.

Venadia signaled for her golden staff which was brought by a young courtier who knelt before her to present it. The Queen thanked the bearer and took it into her grasp using a subtle show of authority as she rose, then descended the steps before her. She joined Blaise and Anara in the power circle.

As her predecessor had done, Venadia spoke the timeless incantation to activate the illusions and energy available to her alone. Without looking about or extending the proceedings with speeches or ceremony, the Queen performed her last official act in the unaffected austere manner which had characterized her reign of The Throne of Council. In a glowing flash of light worthy of Venadia's enemy, the Goddess of Light, the Council chambers disappeared and the transitory field of battle became visible. Venadia withdrew with the others out of range to watch. All that would happen was at hand.

12

In the end it was Aisling MacSweeney and the housekeeper, Bonnie, who were able to keep their wits about them during the aftermath of the tragic multiple deaths at McKinley. With classic Irish sensibility the two women oversaw the almost festive activities of the wake held on the vast grounds behind the mansion. The icy March winds that had howled in mourning for two days had subsided leaving behind a crisp afternoon chill and muted blue skies. Food and libation were in abundance on long tables draped in white and decorated with simple arrangements of lilies.

Bonnie was perpetual motion itself, fussing over everything and everyone. For her, constant activity was the answer to the swell of agony in her heart. If she stayed at it long enough and kept the blood moving through her heart fast enough it wouldn't burst and leave her in a heap of sorrow. She looked upon her activity as her last service to the one she had served since birth.

Aisling was motivated more by her need to protect her daughter, Brigid, who was only functioning from one tranquilizer to the next. Brigid had been torn from her sleep on *that* morning at precisely the moment of Ryan's death. Short of breath and wracked by heart palpitations, somehow Brigid was able to determine that her pain was empathic rather than her own. The horror she'd prayed would never come was upon her; she knew her cousin was dead. Determined, filled with dread, but irresistibly drawn, Brigid had rushed to McKinley. She was not completely surprised by what she (and Bonnie) had found. Advance warning did nothing to lessen the shock of discovering not one but four bodies scarcely gone cold.

Since that devastating moment Brigid, holding on to a fragile line of sanity, occupied herself with carrying out Ryan's instructions to the letter.

The bodies lay in state in front of the elevated podium about which clung the smokey presence of thick incense. As specified, after a brief ceremony the bodies were to be cremated and the ashes stored in a marble vault near the pleasure garden.

Milling about the coffins or seated in the numerous rows of folding chairs facing the podium, the grieving friends and relatives of the deceased talked quietly among themselves. Christine followed Brigid closely, ever at hand to assist her lover with any detail she might find too taxing.

Dealing with the loss of Ryan was an effort Christine was accustomed to making. In one way or another she had been coping with being separated from Ryan for a long time. She'd barely gotten to know Leslie, and Sanji wasn't her favorite person. These deaths couldn't have the emotional impact for her that they did on Brigid; she was free, then, to lend her full capacity for loving to Brigid in her time of great need. Christine's mourning would be done in private, as it always had been.

The other pillar of strength was, not surprisingly, Susan Benson, Leslie's former law partner. To the normally affable Susan fell the difficult task of handling Leslie's estranged relatives. Able to suppress her own feelings, Susan had volunteered to inform "the next of kin" and made herself available to answer their questions about the nature of Leslie's relationship to Ryan and explain why her death had caused the others to choose death also.

In her dealings with the Serle clan Susan learned not to envy Barbara McFarland, the executrix of the wills, and told her as much before the service began. She warned Ryan's attorney to watch for greed and challenges from that heretofore absent group of people. Barbara stoically reassured Susan that, although Leslie didn't expect such behavior from her family, Ryan had and had made certain the wills were incontestable. They shared their disgust over the presence of Leslie's family at the funeral. It was too obvious that, after years of totally ignoring Leslie then suddenly turning out in full force, they were trying to make appearances look good when the time came for the reading of the will. Barbara alone knew they would only receive a token recognition of their bloodties to the Mistress of McKinley.

Other absentee family members who had traveled from abroad to attend the service and pay their respects were the relatives of Sanji and Corelle. They hung back timidly, awed by the grandeur of McKinley and were frightened by the unusual circumstances surrounding the deaths. Simple people from the peasantry of Jamaica and Ireland, they mourned quietly and sincerely. These people Susan ignored, choosing instead to pay particular attention to Charlotte, her former legal secretary, who had been like a mother to Leslie and very much in need of understanding and a good shoulder to cry on.

Another pseudo-relative of Leslie's arrived shortly before the ceremony causing a stir among many women who hadn't seen her for a long time: Star, Brigid's former lover. She, too, was difficult to console, but she behaved graciously to Brigid and Christine. Representative Bennet Waterton was in attendance. He had genuinely liked Leslie and owed his entire career to her; his grief was as heartfelt as was possible when coming from an ambitious man.

A wide range of people from all classes and walks of life found their way to the service because of their association with Ryan over the years: society people, bar people, former employees and business associates, any number of pilots who had worked and flown with Ryan. Marguarita, the art dealer who helped with the plans for the art institute that McKinley was to become, took it upon herself to make those members of society feel at ease in the presence of large numbers of Gay men and Lesbians.

Bernie Valasquez, putting forth a rock-like veneer to mask the devastation she was feeling, likewise stepped forward to settle Ryan's friends from the seamier part of her life. Bernie would later learn that she had inherited Ryan's motorcycle which she would cherish and care for as Ryan had.

But the one person who was inconsolable (which everyone who knew him expected) was Phil Peterson, Ryan's mentor and surrogate father. Only Brigid and Leslie had been closer to Ryan, and no one had spent more time with her. In an effort to acknowledge that relationship, Brigid had given Phil Ryan's leather jacket. Sarah, Phil's wife, had looked on gratefully; the gesture had finally released the barrier between Phil and his tears. He had gone into a kind of emotional shock when he learned of the sad news, leaving him unable to speak or recognize those around him. Sarah, who had been jealous yet fond of Ryan and her place in her husband's heart guided Phil to view the bodies. He stared blankly at Corelle and Sanji; he shook his head and closed his eyes when he viewed Leslie, thinking to himself, what a waste.

Reluctantly he gazed upon his student/friend/comrade—and some said, child, since Ryan had been more like his own than his own. Sarah was worried by the longing "take me with you" expression that masked her husband's face. It wasn't news to Sarah that her husband didn't feel like going on without Ryan; she took him back to his seat in the front row and waited for the service to begin. Phil clutched the jacket closely, staring straight ahead silently, rivulets of tears meandering down his cheeks. (Two years would pass before he would regain his ability to function fully, helped by his family and friends.)

Brigid sat silently behind the podium waiting for the crowd to settle into the rows of chairs on the lawn. She was thankful she'd written down her thoughts the night before; it would have otherwise been impossible to eulogize her friends in the face of so many mourners. Her mother and Christine were seated to either side of her; both were quiet, strong and supportive.

Brigid felt certain she could accomplish this tribute without crying. Surely there weren't any more tears left inside her. She had thought she'd known pain in her life, but none so great as this. She hurt down to her fingertips, was exhausted and numb by turns. A part of her was gone forever, a vitality that she had drawn from Ryan since childhood. The special fire that burned at Ryan's core, sometimes scorching but more often warming and illuminating those in her presence, had been doused. Brigid hadn't realized how often she'd depended on that brilliant fire being there, how many times she'd dipped into that well of energy to keep herself going. Being suddenly forced to cultivate her own reservoir of strength reminded her all the more keenly of her loss.

Looking around her everything seemed lifeless and monochromatic. How could anything look beautiful to her again without Leslie? she had asked herself time and again. More than once in the last three days she had reviled her cousin, calling her a coward for taking her own life. By accident one such malediction had been spoken aloud within Christine's hearing. Christine was quick to point out to Brigid that if she no longer thought the world a place of beauty with Leslie gone, then Ryan would have seen the world as a place without life. When Brigid's suffering and grief lessened, in time, it would be Christine who would show her that the only way to honor Leslie would be to go on creating the beauty Leslie so cherished.

But now, as Brigid rose to deliver the final tribute, color, shape, harmony and rhythm had passed into some unreachable dimension leaving the artist empty and (temporarily) soulless.

The immediate hush of the gathering before her called out to Brigid for succor. All around there was a greater need to understand why this unthinkable tragedy had occurred. Brigid hoped she was up to the task of answering, if only partially, this almost palpable longing that filled the air around her. It was time to say good-bye to these special people who had touched their lives.

Conspicuously absent were Dana and Del and Brigid's own father. Brigid was glad that those three had the graciousness not to soil these proceedings with their hypocrisy.

Sighing hugely, Brigid collected herself to speak. "When the great die there is little to be said to deliver those who remain from the vast empty space their absence creates. How do you bring back a perfect sunset when darkness falls?

"Leslie Anne Serle was the embodiment of all that was beautiful and peaceful in this life. Her presence on this earth made the earth itself a better place to be. For those of us who truly loved her," Brigid stared purposefully in the direction of Leslie's relatives as she paused meaningfully to let them know that *she* knew they had never really loved Leslie, "Leslie was more than just special. She had a quality about her that proved it was possible to be gentle *and* strong. To be Leslie's friend was to be befriended by a queen. Her inner royalty was plain for all to see. She went about her life with courage, truth and dignity. While she would not forgive anyone who hurt someone she loved, her heart was pure and filled with understanding for anyone who hurt her." Brigid lowered her eyes for a moment, remembering how Leslie had forgiven the rape.

Looking up again, fighting off the tears, she forced herself to go on. "Leslie's greatest strength was her courage. It took a great deal of courage to love Ryan O'Donnell. Like her courage, Leslie's love never wavered."   .

Brigid scanned her audience and prayed she was doing the right thing. "Most people find it hard to understand why someone would choose not to live once the one they loved beyond all others had died. In many ways Ryan had no choice. Ryan's life was as tied to Leslie's destiny as was her death. There was simply no reason for Ryan to go on living without Leslie. That's the kind of person Ryan was; she never did anything half-way. She went through this life ruled by her intensity — an intensity that would have ruined any one of us and nearly ruined her. Leslie Serle was the sole reason why Ryan didn't simply self-destruct by collapsing under the weight of her own destiny.

"You couldn't sit on the fence with Ryan, you either loved her or you hated her. Looking at all of you now, I can see that she was well loved." Brigid let her eyes fall on Phil Peterson and her heart warmed to the task. Ryan must be honored — greatly — everyone there deserved that.

"I thought about what one word would best describe the Ryan most of you know. Reviewing her life the same theme repeated itself again and again: generosity. No one needs to be reminded that Ryan was a wealthy woman; it wasn't her who did the reminding. She appreciated her privilege but she never abused it, never made anyone else feel like less of a person if she had less. Ryan never spoke of helping other people but very few weren't the beneficiaries of her generosity. I don't remember when I caught on but it really didn't take much to trace many unexpected good fortunes back to her." Brigid's eyes alighted revealingly on a group of Ryan's bar buddies and she smiled as she watched them nod in agreement. "Hospital bills mysteriously being paid off, jobs suddenly becoming available, businesses financed . . ." Brigid didn't add, "elections won."

"But Ryan gave of herself also. Her time was your time; she didn't turn anyone with a problem away. If she could use her influence, which was considerable," Brigid turned to Christine with a grateful expression, "to change an unfair condition, she did it without thought of recognition or gratitude. One of her most generous gifts to this life is one that will go on in her absence and will keep alive the memory of the one who was dearer to her than life.

"The Serle Art Institute for Women was Ryan's brainchild, the sole issue of her union with her beloved Leslie. Beauty . . ."

Brigid's voice caught in her throat and she found it troubling to go on. She pushed her notes aside for a minute to speak from her heart. "Beauty symbolized Leslie's inner self. It was her gift to us all. The institute has been placed in my charge, its purpose is to create a birthing place for beauty. No greater place could exist — McKinley Mansion is the masterpiece it is today because Leslie made it that way. I can only hope that I will find the strength to see that Ryan and Leslie's dream lives on."

Brigid shifted her weight behind the podium, inhaled deeply and shored herself up to finish. "Sanji Charles and Corelle Trant were unique individuals. They possessed an ability that is not easily recognized or sanctioned in our culture. To serve another human being completely is not a lifestyle that many can accept. Sanji and Corelle did more than accept it, they raised service to an art form. Their service to Ryan and Leslie never went unrewarded. That they were allowed to serve would have been sufficient for either of them; that they were genuinely appreciated and respected was their ultimate reward.

"Personally I only have a sketchy understanding of what motivated these two women. Ryan tried to explain it to me when I asked her about their devotion. In the end I decided that only those who are meant to be served or to serve can truly comprehend the kind of complex relationship Sanji and Corelle had with Ryan and Leslie. Their utter devotion is unquestionable and serves to reinforce in our hearts how special Ryan and Leslie were. Is there more one can do to show one's love than to die, *willingly*, to be with that loved one? I think not. I honor Sanji and Corelle; I know they are happier now, for neither of them would have had a purpose in life if they had remained."

Brigid reached down inside herself for the final draft of courage to keep her wits about her and dignity about this scene. "We must all find a way to say good-bye to these incredible people and thank them for touching our lives, for making life more than what any of us could have lived without them." Tears welled up in Brigid's eyes and her throat constricted. She could barely utter her farewell. "Go in peace, my friends. May your struggle in the life hereafter succeed. I shall cherish your memory for all time."

Brigid stifled a wail and collapsed in her seat. A lone violinist took her place at the podium and performed a Requiem written especially and only for this day. A white dove appeared from nowhere to rest on the podium to listen. When the music ended

131

the crowd dispersed. Brigid thought, no she knew she had seen a tear fall from the dove's eye before it flew away.

"Good-bye, my friends," Brigid murmured, "Good-bye."

13

Blaise eyed Anara warily, taking her measure of this haughty, dangerous adversary. She supposed she should feel some real *desire* to defeat Anara, an urge to covet The Throne and its power, or something that would drive her on. But most of all she wanted a way to fulfill her role without hurting anyone or having anyone hurt. She would have liked it if there had been some precedent for the battle for The Throne being executed without a lot of souls sacrificing their existence before the final outcome. She truly hated Anara, but not so much that she wanted to see her destroyed. Taking a brief look through the mists and flashing colors that surrounded her, she scanned those who were watching and could find no one she would wish obliterated. But the manipulation of power would go on around her while she was squaring off with her opponent with no regard to her reticence.

In the beginning much of what would go on in this battle would occur on a kind of mental plane. To the mortal observer it would appear that nothing was happening but two powerful spirits staring at one another. But, to the initiated, war was going on with a vengeance. Long before either party exhibited any of her actual skills she must be tested to see how she reacted to and responded to the drama going on around her.

Anara had a clear advantage because she was an unfeeling

power-seeking female. In her deepest heart, *everyone* was expendable in her quest for the title of Queen Regent. This was a fact she had managed to keep from all her supporters, even the clever Goddess of Light; who at that very moment was watching for an appropriate time and way to strike out against *her* enemy, the reigning Queen. Her interest heightened when she spied one of Venadia's handmaidens, Lizack, leaving the Queen's side on the trail of a personal vendetta.

Lizack stole away from her honored place at Venadia's left to seek out the elegant man Ramonye. Unlike Blaise, Lizack was not above wanting to see Anara destroyed. Had she possessed the power to eliminate the demi-goddess, Lizack would have done so thousands of years earlier. She felt a genuine satisfaction from being the one who had poisoned Anara's physical self, bringing about her earthly death three millenneums ago. But to destroy another soul . . . that was a different matter. Very few had that power, fewer still were willing to exercise it.

No, the only ways left to Lizack's ilk were trickery and treachery. Lizack's reasoning was simple: go after those close to Anara to weaken her defenses against the unknown powers of Blaise. The Goddess of Light was too clever, the warrioress Caspia was too frightening, and Fila was too dear to Lizack from their earthly sojourn. That left the hermaphrodite and the man. Lizack decided upon the one she was most certain was of some value to Anara, or at least of some help.

Ramonye didn't notice the ebony youth sidling up next to him, she was so quiet. When he did see her he smiled. Lizack coyly returned his smile; she knew he thought himself irresistible to the ladies. And forbidden fruit that she was, Ramonye's attraction to her brightened instantly. Ever bold and sure of himself, he cupped Lizack's shining breast in his hand, fondled it, tweaked the nipple—all this before even speaking to the girl.

Lizack let him handle her, she even pretended to respond to it in an effort to get him to lower his defenses.

"Well, child, what brings you this way? Is not the side of your beloved Mistress a place of honor for you?" Ramonye mocked.

"It is indeed, kind sir." Lizack let her lashes sweep down meekly and she moved encouragingly into his touch. "But she ignores me often," Lizack lied. "I crave excitement, and as you well know, there is little to be had in the presence of so peaceful a Queen."

Ramonye laughed. "Tell me, then, what brings you this way?"

"You," Lizack revealed seductively.

"Why now and not before?" Ramonye quizzed suspiciously.

"Look about you," Lizack replied. "When have I had the chance to do more than admire you from afar? Have you not been engaged with the beautiful Anara? Look yonder at my Mistress. Is she not preoccupied with the proceedings? Which, may I be so bold to assert, might go on for some time? Would not a diversion such as myself help pass this time while you await your Lady's victory?"

"Your questions are well considered, dark child. And you do tempt me. Pray tell what could you possibly gain from such a fancy?" Ramonye already knew that he would take advantage of this rare opportunity to exploit the innocent admiration this seductive servant obviously showed for him. To take a tumble with a Queen's handmaiden was a coup indeed.

"Little," Lizack revealed humbly, "for I know my place is at the side of my Queen; and I could not hope to have for myself a lover as charming and handsome as yourself. But think of the fleeting moment of glory I might carry with me in my heart as I attend the dethroned Queen. How I might relive the happiness in my heart and mind while in the presence of a depressed and unhappy, powerless ruler," Lizack pleaded. She reached out timidly and stroked the rich fabric of Ramonye's robe. Feeling nothing now except disgust, Lizack could tell that the regal man wanted to take her.

Ramonye grinned smugly; he was full of his own attractiveness. "Perhaps you would care to join me in my rooms . . ." he suggested.

Pretending to sound excited, Lizack answered, "You do me honor by suggesting the luxury of being your guest. But I think it would be an unbearable cruelty to allow me such intimacy with no hope of extending it. I know of a secret place we may retire to for a brief time where we might enjoy one another's delights without being missed." Lizack took Ramonye's hand boldly and waited invitingly.

"I see the right of your suggestion. Where . . .?"

"It is not far, kind sir. Please, follow me," Lizack implored. "I beg of you to torment me no longer. I desire you!" Lizack let her gaze dip longingly to fall upon the sight of Ramonye's stiff member forming a tent under his robe.

Unused to such brazenness, Ramonye temporarily forgot his courtly manner and allowed himself to give way to the recklessness of the moment. He followed Lizack down a wide corridor, his steps hurried and light.

Ramonye had to duck to fit under the door Lizack ushered him through. She paused to light a small candle. Letting her hand brush lightly over Ramonye's sex, she encouraged him further. "There are but three turns we must make in these small hallways until we come upon this safe chamber I have spoken of, sir." Without waiting for his reply, Lizack took off down the narrow hall, holding the candle in such a way that it distributed its light over her shapely back and buttocks. Ramonye was not far behind.

Suddenly, she doused the flame and turned to him. "We are here now," she said shakily. "but I grow afraid. Say you will not hurt me. I am not yet used to the ways of men."

Ramonye was now panting with desire and unmindful of his surroundings. "Child, I shall take you with the greatest of care if you so desire it, but it must be now. My passion strains me. Do not be coy or I *shall* hurt you."

Lizack melted into his body. "Very well, sir," she whispered. "Now it shall be. If you will slide past me here and over to the left, you will find the door."

Ramonye moved as she asked. He did not find a door, but a wall which yielded to his weight and spun him around to his left in a ninety degree turn. Instantly he knew he had been tricked. He conjured a ball of spirit light into his hand and looked about him. Lizack was nowhere to be found. On the wall were some markings which he read with mounting horror. He had heard of this ancient place but had never really thought that it existed. Nevertheless he found himself at the beginning of a Labyrinth — a maze wherein all who entered were doomed to endless meanderings and no hope of escape.

The Goddess of Light wasted no opportunity especially ones that were placed so temptingly before her as this one. With Lizack out of sight and the timid Coré relaxing at Venadia's side, there was no better time to strike. And strike she did. The spiteful Goddess hurled a blinding flash of light across the room, aimed directly at the much hated Queen.

Had Coré truly been as relaxed as she appeared and not ever watchful and alert to danger as she was, the deposed ruler would have been burned out of existence. Instead, the faithful childlike handmaiden sprang into action in the same instant the thundering crack of light was sent. It was Coré, not Venadia, who took the full force of the luminous weapon as she threw herself into its path and was smitten down and destroyed for all time.

Blaise's attention was diverted from her battle with Anara by the terror-fraught scream that issued from the normally silent mouth of her beloved. When she looked Venadia's way she was horrified by what she saw. A small pile of ashes lay on the floor before the Queen, and, gathered around her, helping her, were Hestia, Serdon and Pliquay. It appeared that the Goddess of Light had not failed entirely in her assault. Venadia was badly wounded. Scoring her breast and one side of her face were slice marks where the light had burned through the Veils to porcelain skin, sealing the fabric to the skin with ugly, blackened melt marks. One eye seemed ruined, the rest of Venadia's features remained obscured by her everpresent Veils.

Venadia wailed and wept, not for her injury, but for the loss of her dearest and most cherished handmaiden. Hestia drew her near to console her, expressing her love for the Queen and entreating her to quit this dangerous place.

Anara looked on with disgust. The Goddess of Light was nowhere to be seen, but Anara knew where to find her, to reach out mentally to scold the deity. "You fool! Now look what you've done," Anara chastised meanly. "Couldn't you have waited until all this was over to try your clumsy hand at murder? See how angry Blaise becomes. She will be difficult to handle now, you *idiot*. Now I shall have to try a different approach with her altogether, and I was very near having her where I wanted her." Anara snapped off the communication without allowing the absent Goddess to reply. She was now thoroughly put off by her friend and refused to listen to anything the Goddess might say in her defense.

Blaise looked on, near tears. Compassion overrode her anger as she reached out with her mind to console her lover. "My darling, let me come to you! I shall give up this detestable battle to be by your side. Your pain fills me and draws me," Blaise entreated longingly.

Venadia was quick to set aside her pain for the brief moment it took to respond. *"You cannot give up this struggle, Blaise!"* Venadia was weakening rapidly. The force she put behind her plea took precious energy from her. Her voice sounded tiny inside Blaise's mind. "Must I remind you of the destructive nature of Anara and her kind? Look at me. Look at my poor Coré," Venadia sobbed, "a pile of *ashes* where once a vital, faithful being shone brightly . . ."

The Queen was barely able to go on. "I am well cared for. You must concentrate . . ." And stay on guard, the Queen wanted to warn, but she lapsed into a dreamlike state where thought was not easy and communication impossible. Hestia fussed over her anxiously, looking about for Lizack who could help restore the Queen's senses with her strength-giving presence.

"She appears to be well taken care of," Bilouge said sarcastically.

Blaise whipped around to face the hermaphrodite, thinking the creature rude for listening in on her thoughts. Her terse words died aborning when she mentally reassured herself that Bilouge could not have been listening to her private conversation with the Queen. Out of the corner of her eye, Blaise noticed Anara moving the tips of her robes away from the interloper in disgust. It seemed no one felt kindly toward this feathery thing who was the image itself of power gone sour, refinement carried to the ridiculous. Neither Blaise or Anara looked forward to having it serve on any Council she might rule.

Bilouge was quite accustomed to one-sided conversations. "Very well cared for indeed. In fact," it went on, knowing it had Blaise's (and Anara's) attention, "I would not be surprised if our fair Queen were to succumb to the Goddess' solicitous attention and run off with her. The Goddess wouldn't mind if the Queen has lost her beauty." Bilouge purposely drew attention to Anara's great loveliness.

Anara was as clever as she was attractive. She took the unspoken cue by leaning seductively toward Blaise and letting her breasts move into the field of vision of her opponent's incredible red eyes.

Bilouge's thin, grating voice broke the spell Anara was weaving with her body. And not accidently. "Dear Anara, did you know your little toy is no more?" Bilouge inquired, trying to finish what the Goddess of Light had begun. Venadia needed to be gotten rid of. Somehow. Venadia was shoring up Blaise, keeping her interested in the fight she wanted no part of. Bilouge loved court intrigues, and Anara was certain to keep the court intriguing. With Venadia out of the way, Anara was assured of victory.

"What do you speak of, *thing*?" Anara asked derisively.

"Ramonye. Do you see him about?" Bilouge quizzed blandly.

Anara scanned the area quickly then returned her mean stare on Bilouge. "Where is he?" she demanded viciously.

"He has been tricked into the Labyrinth and not even you can release him from his eternal journey to nowhere," Bilouge informed with no small amount of pleasure.

"*How*?" Anara hissed.

"He was led there by . . . ah, here she comes now," Bilouge provided while pointing to Lizack. "The dark handmaiden of our former Queen."

Blaise threw herself on Anara suddenly, but she was too late. The predictable demi-goddess acted quickly by sending spirit-formed knives soaring across space between herself and the unsuspecting Lizack. A millisecond later Lizack was struck down — destroyed — and a loud wail arose from the area where Venadia was being attended.

In a like instant Venadia disappeared, followed closely by Hestia.

"Pity," Bilouge said nastily and walked away — all too proud of its accomplishment.

Blaise pulled herself off Anara and sat down; she was stunned and horrified. Weakly she watched Serdon pick up Lizack's limp form while her lover, Pliquay, reverently gathered the ashes left by Coré's demise and placed the remains safely aside. They knew that if the Queen ever returned, she would want to see that her dear servants would be put to rest in the respectful manner they deserved.

Watching this scene, too, but making a great effort to mask her horror and sadness, was Anara's handmaiden, Fila. The great Amazon had loved Lizack in the physical world. Although here she had no hope of openly expressing that love to Lizack or knowing any reciprocal affection, she could at least comfort herself with the dream of holding Lizack in her arms. Now even *that* dream was dead, and with it died a piece of her innocent devotion to her Mistress.

Little by little it was dawning on Fila that Anara thought her expendable, just another pawn in the the big game Anara was playing to assure herself the crown that awaited the victor of this battle. That Fila could stand there, at attention, thinking such thoughts without Anara noticing was further proof to her that Anara cared nothing for her servant. Had Anara thought of Fila as capable of anything but the slavish love for her, she would have been on guard against awakening awareness in her loyal Amazon. But Anara was too selfish for those kinds of considerations to penetrate her devious mind.

Shrewd combatant that she was, Anara was not above a solicitous approach to her opponent. Gingerly she knelt next to Blaise's motionless form. With extreme care she touched Blaise's shoulder and murmured an apology for her rash actions.

"I am not always one who thinks before acting, Blaise. *You* know that better than any." Anara made her voice sound soft and sincere.

Blaise turned slowly to look at the white-eyed woman. With all her heart she wanted to believe Anara was genuinely sorry for destroying Lizack. When she blinked, tears trailed down her cheeks; she felt abandoned and overwhelmed by loneliness. Venadia had always been there for her, and now she was gone. Where the Queen had disappeared to no one seemed to know. With whom she had disappeared was obvious to everyone. For all intent and purpose it seemed all Blaise had left was Anara. And Anara was being kind to her.

As if reading Blaise's thoughts, Anara pushed to comfort her. "Our former Queen will fare better with the Goddess of Fire who loves her and will not be at all concerned that her beauty is marred." Anara softened her touch still more as she pulled back Blaise's bulky hood to allow her to gaze into her foe's thrilling red eyes. "This ruination and destruction is a waste, Blaise. Let us call an end to it by sharing The Throne. We can rule together in harmony — as one," Anara suggested cunningly in an attempt to take advantage of Blaise's reluctance to destroy anyone.

The dark warrioress, Caspia, moved into position next to her kinswoman, the Amazon Fila. Her voice rolled like thunder but Fila was not startled by it. "This scene sickens me and makes my entrails squeeze. There was a time when I would have welcomed even Blaise as Queen Regent to rid us of the softness of the Veiled One," Caspia vilely spat out Venadia's informal title letting her rugged face contort into a crude look of disgust. Receiving only an impassive acknowledgement to her statement

140

from Fila, she spoke on. "But it is clear that only Anara has the strength we need to lead the Council. Blaise is weak," Caspia scorned. "Even now she does not see that Anara is setting her up."

Fila's attention snapped away from the goings on before her and shifted urgently to her kinswoman. Caspia gave a long, thoughtful look at her hardened, bronze friend. "Ah, love *has* blinded you, fellow warrior. It has been too long since you have been seasoned in the field. Even the motives of those closest to you go unnoticed."

The impatient expression on Fila's fine face warned Caspia that, while she had been away from her craft for some time, she was still as quick and dangerous as ever.

Caspia elaborated for her friend. "Anara has no intention of sharing The Throne with Blaise or anyone else. The first opportunity she gets, she'll do away with Blaise. And if she doesn't," Caspia threatened, "I will. I will not serve two Queens," she stated hatefully. "Look you there," Caspia drew Fila's gaze to Blaise and Anara walking toward them. Blaise's resigned appearance showed Fila all she needed to see but had refused to: Blaise's apparent weakness was truly her strength. Here was a being who could forgive wrongdoings, was without rank ambitions, who would only destroy if forced to and then only if all alternatives failed. Blaise was true, that Fila knew as she recalled what they had shared in the physical world and how Blaise had forgiven her all the cruelly unjust acts she had committed in Anara's name.

As she watched Blaise sluggishly walking along in front of Anara, who hung back, Fila's heart was filled with the pain of losing Lizack. It was with that intense realization Fila was able to act without hesitation. The moment Blaise passed by her, Fila was able to see the intent in her Mistress' eyes. The uncanny strength and reflexes that marked her race gave Fila all that she needed to be in the right place at precisely the instant Anara struck. She leapt into the path of the oncoming flash of pure energy that had been designed to destroy Blaise. Fila's action saved Blaise not once by twice. By taking the strike meant for Blaise, Fila saved her from the first, betraying dagger of energy. Her cry of pain alerted Blaise to the second, more deadly assault.

Instinctively Blaise bespoke her own name of power which transformed her at will into a flashing wall of flame. Her fiery state was indestructible and through it passed Anara's bolt of energy. Equally harmless was Caspia's mighty spear which also passed through the flames and fell to the ground beyond.

No one present had ever seen Blaise attack anyone or anything before. Anara and Caspia were not on guard against the blaze as it gathered speed and began to twist into a vortex. Without warning the whirling mass leapt across the distance and descended upon Anara engulfing her in its burning cylinder. Anara's screams of unbearable pain were swallowed by the flames as light is swallowed by darkness. She was thus sealed in a capsule of transparent fire and, standing next to her now, in all her glowing glory, was her fierce, angry opponent.

Blaise spun around to point a threatening finger at the warrioress. *"Try it*, Caspia," Blaise warned dangerously.

Caspia halted mid-stride, her sword poised. Her calculating eyes darted from Blaise's shimmering grey form to the column of fire where Anara could be seen as she writhed and churned in pain, her mouth forming unheard pleas for surcease. This, then, was a display of what the red-eyed melancholic contender was capable of when pressed, Caspia assured herself as she thought better of her attack.

Slowly, her sword lowered and she stepped out of her crouch and turned to salute the air where Fila had once stood. Bringing her fist soundly to her chest, she paid tribute to her kinswoman who had fallen in the struggle for what she believed, in the end, to be the right way. Blaise bowed her head silently in respect, then disappeared.

Alone in the private place where, over the eons, she had gone to seek comfort, love and guidance from her beloved mate, Blaise sat quietly. She was shaken to her very foundation. How had all this come about? How had she been abandoned, betrayed and nearly destroyed, all in so brief a time? She mulled over Fila's selfless act and wondered how the Amazon had changed her viewpoint so suddenly. She stood and began to pace, trying to decide what to do with Anara. She was loathe to destroy her opponent and wanted to find a way around that choice.

These were problems that could be solved in time, she knew, but what of the loneliness? Hadn't she forsaken Venadia in the not too distant past? How could she now ask that pure spirit to return from the arms of the Goddess who loved her? But to go on without Venadia . . . how could she? The impasse was impassable. She was locked in battle with herself. Suddenly she was overcome by the desperation of her situation and she cried out: "VENADIA . . .!"

The painful cry of her name pierced Venadia's heart with a searing ache that burned many times more than the grief that saturated her being. She brought her hand to her heart to hold it fast lest it burst wide open with suffering. Hestia pulled the Queen close and questioned her. "What is it, dearest? Not more pain . . .?" the Goddess asked with amazement. Surely there couldn't be anything to bring more trouble to this glorious woman unless . . . "Say it isn't so. Blaise cannot have . . ."

Venadia stood quickly. "She exists still, but she needs me. Now. I must go to her, Hestia. I thank you for your healing attentions, but I can think of myself no longer."

Before the Goddess could voice her objections, the Queen was gone.

Into the mists and hum of peace that surrounded the gentle sanctuary Blaise and Venadia had created for themselves materialized the beautiful and perfect form of the Veiled One, Venadia. Softly she knelt and touched Blaise's hunched over and sobbing form.

"My darling," she greeted sweetly.

Slowly, wiping away her tears, Blaise raised up, letting her eyes reluctantly follow the Veils upwards to greet her mate. With astonishment and great gladness she smiled and sighed with heavy relief. "You are well," she breathed happily, for Venadia was whole and healed as completely as one with a broken heart can be. Her wounds were no longer evident.

"Hestia has been kind to me. Her attentions and devotion were most effective."

"You have not become Hestia's consort?" Blaise asked with wonder.

Venadia raised her Veils to reveal her polished ivory face and

143

smiled. "No, my love. Although Hestia would wish it otherwise, I am yours alone. I am sorry if I have done anything to cause you to doubt that for even a moment." Venadia took Blaise's oval-shaped face into her hands and drew her near. Her earnest and genuine love melted the pain and sternness from her golden eyes as she looked softly into Blaise's searching red orbs.

Scarcely believing Venadia was really in her arms, Blaise let her wine-tinted lips caress the Queen's receptive yellow mouth. Easily, but on the verge of electrifying passion, the lovers rid one another of all garments, moaning, moving together in the harmony that only those who have been together since creation itself could. Their private knowledge of their selves singularly and as a duo was matchless in its perfection. They reaffirmed, reassured, renewed, restored all that was their love for and bond with the other. Their mating was a celebration filled with desire, power and bliss. The emptiness, loneliness and loss were scorched clean by the fires of their need.

Completion and fulfillment settled over the couple like a soft blanket of warm fur, relaxing them and giving them the strength they would need to go on. They lay entangled in one another's arms relishing their familiarity and peace.

In due time they dressed, their eyes bespeaking their oneness. Refreshed, they could attend to the matters at hand with a soundness that came from the best part of themselves.

"You have destroyed Anara," Venadia speculated quietly.

Blaise sighed heavily and shook her head sadly. "No, I haven't, Venadia, I just couldn't bring myself to do it," she declared with frustration.

Venadia was surprised and showed it. "Blaise, you *must*. It is the only way to assure that you can rule The Throne. She cannot be trusted," Venadia insisted.

Blaise thought of how the demi-goddess had already betrayed her, but her reluctance to destroy another being entirely showed clearly on her face.

Venadia softened her approach. Taking Blaise's hand in hers she spoke with restraint. "Think of my Lizack and Coré. They gave their very beings to protect me and assist you in your struggle."

Blaise closed her eyes against the pain. "And Fila, she too has sacrificed her soul to protect me," Blaise revealed.

"Oh, Blaise," the Queen offered sympathetically. Her eyes

were nearly begging when she urged Blaise to look into them as she asked, "Are their sacrifices to be in vain, then?"

No longer able to avoid the inevitable or the truth, Blaise shook her head solemnly. If for no other reason than to honor those who gave their essences to advance the cause, Blaise agreed to follow her destiny.

When Blaise and Venadia returned to the battle ground they found several interested parties waiting for them. Pliquay and Serdon, Caspia and Bilouge and, because the presence of a Goddess was required to witness the passing of one of the contenders, Hestia stood for her deified sisters (the Goddess of Light had yet to return from her sulk).

With grim determination, Blaise turned to the cocoon of flames she had Anara pitilessly trapped in. It was obvious to everyone who looked on that finishing off Anara was little more than an act of mercy. The demi-goddess was a hollow shell of agony, no longer a reasoning being. In a flash it was over. Blaise had willed her elemental flames to do her bidding and consume the remains of her opponent. A small char mark was all that was left once the deed was done.

Venadia nodded her head approvingly. She alone knew what Blaise was feeling. It was an ugly business fighting for The Throne, but one well worth the pleasureless task. As Queen Regent, Blaise would be able to use the power that would be conferred upon her to manipulate the events on Earth to the good of all. Blaise's sensitivity and lack of personal ambition would keep her motives free of pettiness and greed. She would in time learn to rule with a sure, steady hand and capitalize on her strengths while protecting her weaknesses. Yes, Blaise would do The Throne justice, Venadia thought to herself.

The others retired to the Council chambers without fanfare. Venadia took her lover's hand. "Come, my darling, my Queen. Your Council requests your presence."

Epilogue

The ancient chambers were bright and fresh. Garlands of flowers decorated the walls, filling the room with a soothing scent. All the members of the Council took their seats; Blaise invited Hestia, the Goddess of Fire, to take the seat left vacant by the missing Ramonye, and Hestia accepted.

The Goddess of Light took her place next to the warrioress, appearing for all as unruffled and well-behaved as a young maid at court. It seemed there was no real love lost in Anara's defeat.

Blaise was relaxed now, and no longer in fear of danger to herself or Venadia. The destruction was over; it was business as usual, and all animosity was set aside until such a time as it was outgrown or the next battle for The Throne took place. Deities were as long on patience as they were on memory.

Tradition held that if the previous Queen survived she was required to pass her symbol of power on to her successor in a simple, dignified manner. Venadia did so by escorting Blaise to the power circle and handing the staff reverently and lovingly to her mate. Blaise closed her eyes slightly and received the golden rod with a carefully restrained authoritative action that would characterize her reign.

All rose and watched as Blaise ascended the steps, then turned to face her Council. Once the courtier formally proclaimed her as the new Queen Regent, she took her seat upon

The Throne. It was neither an exhilarating nor fearful moment; it was simply a feeling of rightness, of order and contentment. Indeed, this *was* where she belonged and she no longer fought against it. Her acceptance of her new role shone about her and she put forth her staff in the ceremonial gesture that signalled her readiness to accept the allegiance of each member of the Council.

One by one they stepped forward and touched the golden ball of the staff and bowed before their new Queen. It was at this time that a member could chose to stand down from her seat, but none did. Blaise had shown herself able to serve as a true ruler whom they could respect and work with.

Now that the Council was a whole entity once more, Blaise rose to speak.

"I wish to make my first official act a joyous one. I ask all here to join me as I preside over the festivities already in progress outside our Chambers. Let us turn our attentions to a happy occasion and go forward with the ascension ceremonies to install our former Queen as the Goddess of Peace." Blaise drew everyone's attention to the Veiled One and a cheer arose from all.

"Hear, hear," they cried happily. It was a time for a long, carefree, hedonistic festival where everyone, including Venadia, could let go and enjoy.

GLOSSARY OF NAMES

Aisling MacSweeney — Brigid MacSweeney's mother.

Anara — In past lifetime three thousand years ago she was High Priestess of a Pagan clan.
    In spirit world she is a demi-goddess bent on revenge against the members of her clan who were responsible for her death. She is in contention for the title of Queen Regent of the Throne of Council. Name of growth: The Contender. Name of power: Anara.

Bilouge — Member of Council.

Blaise — In an earlier lifetime she was Korian, Anara's lover and apprentice to become High Priestess.
    In current lifetime she is Ryan O'Donnell, Leslie's lover.
    In spirit world she is Anara's opposition to the title of Queen Regent of the Throne of Council. She is Venadia's lover. Name of growth: Woman of Wings. Name of power: Blaise.

Bonnie — The woman who helped Patrick O'Donnell raise Ryan; head of Ryan's household staff.

Brigid MacSweeney — Ryan's cousin and best friend; Star's lover.

Caspia — Warrioress; Member of Council.

Christine Latham — Young woman who had an illegal love affair with Ryan.

Corelle — Leslie's personal servant and handmaiden.

Dana Shaeffer — Ryan's ex-lover, Delores Rhinehart's current lover, Brigid's mistress.

Delores Rhinehart — Leslie's former law partner, Dana's lover.

Fila — Anara's handmaiden in former life three thousand years past.

In recent lifetime she was Rags, serving as Anara's agent of revenge.

In spirit world she is Anara's handmaiden.

Goddess of Fire — Exists in the spirit world and is in love with Venadia. Name of power: Hestia.

Goddess of Light — Member of Council; Venadia's arch-enemy.

Hestia — Goddess of Fire's name of power.

Korian — In lifetime three thousand years past she was Anara's lover and apprentice to become High Priestess of the Pagan clan.

In current lifetime she is Ryan O'Donnell, Leslie's lover.

In spirit world she is Blaise, Venadia's lover, Anara's opposition to the title of Queen Regent of the Throne of Council. Name of growth: Woman of Wings. Name of power: Blaise.

Leslie Anne Serle — Ryan's lover. Three thousand years ago, in a past life, she was Korian's mother.

In the spirit world she is the current holder of the title of Queen Regent of the Throne of Council; Blaise's lover. Name of growth: One Who Seeks Knowledge and Justice. Name of power: Venadia.

Lizack — In her existence three thousand years ago she was in love with Korian and was the one who murdered Anara.

In her current lifetime she is Ryan's sex-slave Sanji.

One Who Seeks Knowledge and Justice — Venadia's (Leslie's) name of growth. Current holder of the title of Queen Regent of the Throne of Council. Blaise's (Ryan's) lover.

Patrick O'Donnell — Ryan's deceased father.

Phil Peterson — Ryan's aviation mentor, business partner and father figure.

Pliquay — Member of Council.

Rags — In her first former life she was Fila, Anara's hand-maiden in the Pagan clan.

In her most recent life existence (as Rags) she was Ryan's friend and persecutor. She was sent by Anara to destroy Ryan's will and failed.

In the spirit world she is Fila, Anara's handmaiden.

Ramonye — Member of Council.

Ryan O'Donnell — Central figure. Three thousand years ago she was Korian, Anara's lover and protege.

In her current life she is Leslie's lover and Anara's enemy.

In the spirit world she is Blaise, Venadia's (Leslie's) lover and Anara's opposition to the title of Queen Regent of the Throne of Council. Name of growth: Woman of Wings. Name of power: Blaise.

Sanji Charles — In her former life she was Lizack who was in love with Korian and was the one who murdered Anara.

In her current lifetime she is Ryan's sex-slave and Leslie's handmaiden.

Serdon — Member of Council.

Susan Benson — Leslie's former law partner.

Bernie Valasquez — Ryan's friend and employee.

Venadia — In a former life she was Korian's mother.

In her current life she is Leslie, Ryan's lover.

In the spirit world she is the current holder of the title of Queen Regent of the Throne of Council. Name of growth: One Who Seeks Knowledge and Justice. Name of power: Venadia.

OTHER BOOKS
OF INTEREST

THE RAGING PEACE, by Artemis OakGrove, $9.00. Love, anger, and desire bring together Leslie, a lawyer, and Ryan, a skilled pilot who grieves for her father. (Volume I of The Throne Trilogy)

DREAMS OF VENGEANCE, by Artemis OakGrove, $9.00. Leslie and Ryan's love is tested again by the goddess Anara who manipulates their sex slaves, Sanji and Corelle. (Volume II of The Throne Trilogy)

THRONE OF COUNCIL, by Artemis OakGrove, $9.00. Ryan's and Leslie's earthly and spiritual lives collide, and each must decide in which they will choose to live. (Volume III of The Throne Trilogy)

TRAVELS WITH DIANA HUNTER, by Regine Sands, $8.00. When 18-year-old Diana Hunter runs away from home she begins an odyssey of love, lust, and humor spanning almost twenty years.

ALARMING HEAT, by Regine Sands, $8.00. More tales of lesbian sexual adventures from the author of *Travels with Diana Hunter*.

MACHO SLUTS, by Pat Califia, $10.00. A stunning collection of erotic short fiction which explores a wide variety of sexual situations and fantasies.

THE LESBIAN S/M SAFETY MANUAL, edited by Pat Califia, $8.00. An essential guide for leather dykes who want to learn how to play safe.

COMING TO POWER, edited by SAMOIS, $10.00. An exploration of the world of lesbian sadomasochism.

Ask for these books at your favorite bookstore. If not available locally, they may be ordered by mail from Alyson Publications, 40 Plympton St., Boston, MA 02118. Enclose $1.00 postage with your order.